Freewill may be an illusion but Evil is very real

a Novella
ABHUMAN
THE COVENANT
By:
Hugh B. Long

Published by: Asgard Studios
Ottawa, Canada
www.asgard-studios.com

Tarbizhad™ and **Skaduwee**™ are Trademarks of Hugh B. Long

ISBN: 978-1-927646-68-7

Library and Archives Canada Cataloguing in Publication

Long, Hugh B., author
  Abhuman : the covenant / Hugh B. Long.

Issued in print and electronic formats.
ISBN 978-1-927646-66-3 (hardback).--ISBN 978-1-539178-76-7
(paperback).--
ISBN 978-1-927646-69-4 (GooglePlay epub).--ISBN 978-1-927646-62-5
(Kindle mobi).--
ISBN 978-1-927646-65-6 (Kobo epub)

  I. Title.

PS8623.O5345A63 2016   **C813'.6**
C2016-907060-3

C2016-907061-1

For Kim

(Guild Momma)

Also by Hugh B. Long

The Yggdrasil Codex: Book 0

Star Wolves - The Tribes of Yggdrasil: Book 1

Star Fury - The Tribes of Yggdrasil: Book 2

Star Viking - The Tribes of Yggdrasil: Book 3

A Relatively Nice Place

Want more free books and stories?

Signup for my new releases updates, and you can download more free stories!

Go to this link to subscribe: http://goo.gl/zYa6IF

Like Norse Mythology & Viking Culture?

Check out my non-fiction books written as Eoghan Odinsson:

Northern Lore - A Field Guide to the Northern Mind, Body, and Spirit

Northern Wisdom: The Havamal, Tao of the Vikings

Northern Plant Lore: A Field Guide to the Ancestral Use of Plants in Northern Europe

The Runes in 9 Minutes

About the Author

Hugh B. Long is an Award Winning Canadian Journalist and Best Selling Author. He writes full time, and is passionate about Science Fiction and Fantasy rooted in Mythology. He also writes Norse and Viking themed non-fiction under the pen name – Eoghan Odinsson.

Graduating from the University of Aberdeen's School of Engineering in Scotland with his Masters of Science degree, he subsequently taught for the University, and was a dissertation advisor for graduate students.

In addition to his academic background, Hugh also holds a Black Belt in Shito-Ryu Karate, a Brown Belt in Budoshin Ju-Jitsu, and was study group leader in D.C. for the ARMA (Historical European Martial Arts). Hugh has taught Martial Arts in Canada and the USA.

He has recently returned from a 10 year stretch working in the Washington D.C. area, and is now back in his native Ottawa Valley where he lives with his wife, son and two dogs.

THE COVENANT

AS SHIP MORNING DAWNED, CHESKA Bellamy was looking baffled at the alien landscape stretching out before her. The sky bathed her in pink light, hues of red and blue dancing above a rust colored plain. Weathered rocks and low mountains framed the landscape.

Looking down, she noticed her feet were bare. Purple grass poked up between her toes; patches of it lay scattered over the surface. She only knew it was grass from qvids she'd experienced, and of course the artificial scents pumped into the air above ground level. Cheska had never set foot on any planet in her entire life.

Too shocked to move, she turned her head to soak up the landscape. The sky above her hung black, full of stars, though she could see around perfectly, despite no moon or artificial light. It was like being caught between times—somewhere in the space where night and dawn met in passing.

She stood in a valley or canyon of some kind. Reddish cliffs rose up to surround her, while clumps of purple grass provided some contrast. How could this be real? Was she dreaming?

She still held a glass of milk and took a swig out of habit. Her face contorted as her mind registered that the milk was sour. She promptly spat it all over the grass. Nobody dreamed something that real, did they?

A boy, looking similarly confused, appeared at the other end of the canyon—perhaps a couple of hundred meters away. He walked toward her.

Cheska wanted to run, but she was also intensely curious. The boy might have been around her age, or a bit older. Seventeen or eighteen, maybe? He had thick black hair and piercing almond eyes tinged with a hint of fear.

"Are we dreaming?" she asked him.

He said nothing, looking too stunned to respond.

"My name is Cheska," she said, tapping her chest— in case he didn't speak common. "Cheska Bellamy"

"I--I'm Taro Maki. Where are we?" he asked.

Cheska shook her head slowly. "I have no idea. I thought I was dreaming." She had an idea, and closed the distance so she stood at arm's length to him. She handed him the half-full glass of sour milk. "Smell this."

He leaned down tentatively, sniffed, then recoiled with a shudder. "It's bad!"

Cheska nodded. "I know."

Taro scowled. "Then why did you ask me to smell it?"

"To see if we're dreaming, of course. We can't both be dreaming about my sour milk."

His scowl slowly morphed into a smile. It was a handsome smile. "Probably not."

Cheska gestured to the heavens above. "Do you recognize any of the stars?" She asked more to test Taro, as she specialized in gravitics and was well acquainted with local astronomy.

Taro looked up. "Yes. There." He pointed to a grouping of seven stars. "The Savior's Sword."

She stared at it for a moment. "Right. Ok, I recognize that now. So, we're on Krijese?"

"Have to be," Taro said.

"But this valley …" she said, motioning around to the grass. "It shouldn't look like this. Not yet, anyhow. Not for years. The terraforming isn't complete."

Taro turned and stared of into the distance. "Do you see that?" He pointed at some distant figures moving along the horizon.

Cheska strained her eyes, and, as if she'd zoomed in with an optical aid, the figures appeared larger, seeming barely a stone's throw away. She lurched back, as did Taro. Four humanoids; two large, and two small, walked hand in hand. They appeared vaguely reptilian, their skin a matte green with meter-long ovoid heads tapering back. The creatures didn't seem to notice Cheska or Taro, and continued their casual walk.

"What are they?" Taro asked.

Cheska shook her head, too stunned to speak. She watched them walk with a peculiar gait, their knees bent backward, like those of dogs—which she'd only seen in qvids.

"Maybe this isn't Krijese," Taro said. "Our surveyors reported no life forms on Krijese, else-wise we'd have never started terraforming, right?"

Cheska somehow knew that it was Krijese. Just not the Krijese of their time—the battered and scarred Krijese. It was the planet the Artaldeans had battled and beat down into submission. She was seeing into the past … but how?

"Taro, I think that- " Cheska began.

Taro opened his mouth to speak, but he faded like smoke caught in a stiff wind. As Taro disappeared, Cheska's kitchen reappeared.

Cheska's mother was staring at her. "Cheska, are you feeling ill?" Her mother pressed the back of her hand on Cheska's forehead. "You don't feel hot."

She was still a bit disoriented, then saw the reason for her mother's concern—Cheska hadn't spat the sour milk on grass, she'd spat it all over the kitchen floor.

"Sorry, Mum." Was all she managed. Her mind raced away from spilled milk.

***

Cheska lived with her mother in Ngome City on the terraforming starship *Ghimorphos*. The ship was an enormous sphere, five-kilometers in diameter. Nine domed city habitats, each one-kilometer across, bloomed on the outside of the sphere.

The *Ghimorphos* was currently assigned to breathe life

into a planet called Krijese. The mission had actually begun nearly a century earlier, but would be finished in Cheska's lifetime. Her children were to be the seeds of a new civilization.

Titanic skyscrapers soared above her, a few almost bursting through the top of the dome at 500 meters. The elite lived up in those great towers, while the more common folk, like Cheska and her mother, lived below the surface. She was headed down, not up.

She took a last breath of the fresh air; one more lungful infused with artificial hints of jasmine and fresh cut grass—the air beneath street level was not pre-processed quite so sweetly. Below the majesty of the great buildings and elegant spires, even the air was more humble, scented with hydraulic fluid, burnt energy packs, and the subtle aroma of corroding metal.

She picked her way slowly beneath the roots of the great structures, ducking down into the bowels of the city and its tangle of passageways. Below the living quarters, past ducts and drains, around corners and twists and turns, she wound through the sub-level maze to her secret place.

Cheska arrived at the end of a tunnel and the edge of the dome, its surface smooth and opaque, except for a small patch no larger than her head. This patch was as clear as glass.

She pressed her hands and face against the cold of the dome, staring across the inky black of space, marveling at the planet below. From orbit, the planet Krijese looked like a glass marble; swirls of rusty brown and red mixed with splotches of cobalt blue. It was hypnotic.

Cheska and her best friend, Azara Misra, came to this spot often—it was the only section of the dome that didn't have artificial sky or walls projected on it—some kind of glitch maybe. Whatever the reason, it provided the girls their own private window into a new world. Not only could they see the planet Krijese below, but they could also see three of the other nine domed city habitats.

"Hey there, Red!" came her friend Azara's voice.

Cheska turned to scowl at Azara, who delighted at coming up with new nicknames. Red was the latest, and least inspired, in a growing line of monikers for Cheska and her red hair.

"Hello, *Azara*," she said with mock seriousness.

"Greetings, *Cheska*," Azara returned in an equally ominous tone.

They grinned and hugged—they always hugged. Azara Misra was more than a friend—like a sister. They were inseparable.

"See anything new today?" Azara asked

"Maybe." Cheska pointed to Krijese. "See there. I think that lake—or ocean—has gotten bigger."

"Hmm," Azara said, pressing her hands on the dome and staring out, "maybe." She turned back to Cheska. "But … on to more important things. Did your mother buy your confirmation dress yet?"

Cheska rolled her eyes. "I'm trying to show you a new ocean on a blossoming planet, and you want to talk dresses?"

"Um, yeah?" Azara said, cocking her head.

"Confirmation of Purity comes once in a person's lifetime. Kind of important?"

Cheska shot Azara a pout. She didn't really want to dwell on her impending doom—tomorrow would be her sixteenth birthday. A kiloton of baggage went along with that—such as the Confirmation of Purity.

"You worried?" Azara asked.

"No. Not really." But it was a lie, a secret she desperately wanted to share with her best friend. But she couldn't risk it. Sharing that secret would kill her and put her mother's life in jeopardy as well. She had to be ever vigilant of accidentally triggering her *episodes*. If her people knew what she was, she'd be sent to the Core —said to be a place of damnation where deviants would burn for all eternity. She shuddered at the thought. The Confab preached that aberrations like her were a sin, and the work of demons called Skads; said to corrupt mortals, offering them power in exchange for their souls. She shoved those morbid thoughts to the farthest corner of her mind, determined not to let those worries dominate her day.

Azara grinned. "You'll be just fine. I've known you all my life and you've never seemed anything but ordinary."

"Gee, thanks!" Cheska said.

Azara rolled her eyes. "You know what I mean."

"I do." Cheska stared back out toward Krijese. "I wish my Dad were here to see it. The planet, I mean. He was so proud of what we were building."

Azara set a hand on Cheska's shoulder. "He'd be proud of you too."

Cheska place a hand over the green gem that hung in a pendant around her neck; the last gift she'd ever received from her father. She smiled when she remembered how he'd told her that because the gem matched her eyes it was supposed to be good luck. Yeah, he would have been proud, she thought.

***

"Mum, I'm home!" Cheska announced, as she strolled into their subsurface quarters. The walls were rusted, several layers of paint flaking here and there, where families long before her's had attempted to freshen things up. Their quarters were clean though, her mother insisted on that. They couldn't do much about rust, but they could be clean and tidy.

She didn't see her mother. She poked her head into her Mum's bedroom, then into the dining room— nothing. As she turned around, she gasped to see her mother standing behind her holding up a white gown.

"Skads! Are you trying to scare me to death before my confirmation?" Cheska asked.

"What do you think?" Her mother asked, handing her the dress.

Cheska was truly awed, taking it tentatively. The glittering white gown looked like it must have been spun by tiny hands. Its diaphanous lace was quite a contrast to the slate grey coveralls her mother wore. She had no words for long seconds, but finally spoke. "You … made this?"

Eliza Bellamy nodded, her short, auburn hair bobbing. "Of course. We couldn't afford to buy one this nice." Cheska had always wanted hair like her mother's

—auburn was still sort of red, but not quite. Cheska wondered what color her genetic mother's hair was, or, had been. Or her genetic father's, for that matter. Information on one's genetic parents was a Covenant secret.

Cheska very carefully hung the dress by a hanger on a cupboard handle, then threw herself at her mother, squeezing her for all she was worth. She'd told her mother and Azara that she didn't care what she wore to the ceremony, but that had been a lie—of course she cared. Though she accepted their humble station in life, she still wanted others to think she at least cared about her appearance. And there would be 147 other sixteen-year-old boys and girls going through the ceremony. Confirmation of Purity was held four times a year for boys and girls turning sixteen, or close to it. Days after the ceremony, those new adults would start their grown up lives, entering an intensive training program and moving into co-ed living quarters.

"Thanks, Mum," she whispered.

Eliza rubbed Cheska's shoulders. "You're most welcome, daughter. Your father would have been proud of you."

Cheska cast her gaze to the floor, but nodded.

Eliza placed kiss on Cheska's cheek. "I have to run. Off to work."

"I thought you were off tonight?" Cheska asked. She worried about her mother, who looked haggard these days. Her once clear blue eyes seemed faded, appearing more grey. Streaks of her hair seemed to be following suit.

"Some problem with water reclamation in one of the towers. I have to make sure the sky-people can water their flowers. Shouldn't be too long. Why don't you invite Azara over for dinner?"

"Maybe."

"Bye, love," her mother said, as the door to their quarters whisked closed.

Alone again, she mused. Much of the time she embraced solitude, but then there were times, like now, when she yearned to hear her mother's voice, or even just her footsteps in the kitchen—some token to remind her she was not alone. She got this way when she thought about her Dad. She'd been a daddy's girl. Even following in his footsteps through a career in engineering; though he had specialized in genetic engineering, while her passion lay with gravitics.

Then had come the accident. Apparently, there had been a containment breach in the lab and her father had been exposed to a deadly viral agent. Cheska had only been four-years-old at the time. She'd attended his funeral, but never really got to say goodbye—she and her mother hadn't been allowed to see the body.

The funeral was supposed to have provided her with closure—that's what the therapist had called it. Funerals were supposed to do that.

It hadn't.

***

Cheska dragged herself out of bed after a fitful sleep. Today was the day. She was sixteen—a new adult. That morning she was scheduled for her first orientation session. Her head swam with the competing forces of pure dread and exhilaration.

She shuffled down the corridor to her mother's room, but the neatly made bed told her that she was already gone to work—again. She allowed herself a moment of self-pity at waking alone on her birthday, but shook it off. She'd see her mother later.

A quick breakfast consumed, she hesitated before leaving their quarters. Great Savior—this was it. The door hissed open.

The underbelly of Ngome City was normally crowded and bustling, but not as much today. She took a deep breath and started walking.

***

At six-years-old, Cheska had tested very high in applied physics and quantum mechanics. That had put her on a ten year track to an engineering maintenance career. She'd just learned a few days before that she'd been awarded a prestigious posting in gravitic engineering, where she would maintain the artificial gravity and contragrav systems on the *Ghimorphos*.

The next two days were to be orientation for her new life as an adult—to help ease her into the working world, as it were. Sure, she'd done some co-op as a part of her training, but she'd be leaving home to live in a pod with co-workers, and soon, her old life would be but a memory. New things were exciting, but they also scared her.

"Hey there, kiddo," came the deep baritone of her friend, Jakande Boro.

The voice caught Cheska by surprise since she was still deep in thought about Taro and the dream.

She smiled when she turned to see a huge form towering over her's. Jak was captain of the Watchers—they kept the peace. He was also kind of a self-appointed big brother to Cheska.

"You can't call me kiddo anymore, old man," Cheska said.

He shrunk back, cringing. "Old man? You wound me." He straightened, a tender smile forming on his face. "Happy birthday, young woman."

Cheska rolled her eyes. "Thanks. I guess."

Jak grinned. "You still have time for Gravma practice later?"

Cheska's eyebrows shot up. "Definitely, I'm going to have to start fighting off potential suitors now."

"Right ... I forgot about that part."

"I didn't. Let me assure you."

At sixteen, new adults were encouraged to start getting ready for pairing the following year. Essentially, they had one year to sample the available gene pool—that thought made Cheska shudder. At the end of the year they were paired up with a life-partner. Sometimes their wishes were considered, but genetic compatibility trumped preference. If she were being honest, she was dreading the prospect. What if she fell in love? Then wasn't paired with that person? Yeah, that would suck! But she knew the system was in place for a reason. With an insular population like that of the *Ghimorphos*, inbreeding had always been a risk. Her ancestors had taken extreme precautions—the ship's computers calculated the best genetic pairing, then the female's eggs and the male's sperm were harvested, combined, and the fertilized egg implanted in a totally different female. That way, the colonists were all one big family. Parents raised children, just not their own biological children. It seemed to work. Everybody was healthy and happy … mostly.

The thing that was always in the back of Cheska's mind, and a something she had yet to come to terms with, was the fact that she *had* to do this. She'd been taught that Artaldeans had freewill. How could she have freewill when she would be forced to pair with someone —for life? The thought made her skin crawl! She was trapped.

Jak put on his serious face. "If any of those boys give you a hard time, you call me up? Ok? I mean it."

She nodded. She knew he meant it. She wasn't sure why Jak had ever unofficially adopted her as a little sister, but she was sure glad he had.

"Gotta go, Jak. Need to learn how to adult." Cheska forced a smile as she jogged off down the passageway.

***

Cheska felt a tingling deep inside her brain and slowed down abruptly. Intense activities triggered her episodes, which always began and ended with a mild tingling sensation.

When she'd hit puberty, along with all the other womanly challenges, she'd started having the bursts of speed. It was like she moved faster, or the world slowed down. The first time she'd been alone in her mother's quarters while she was at work. Cheska had been about to walk across the living room to reach for a vase of flowers on a bookshelf, when she ran smack into the shelf, toppling the vase and several of her mother's ornaments. It was like she'd been shoved.

The implications had terrified her. She'd been a wreck for the rest of the day, deflecting her mother's concern by saying it was just boy trouble. And in fact, that had been partly true, a boy whom she'd never met was also part of her problem. A few weeks earlier she'd started having dreams about a boy—not dreams really, more like visions. She even knew his name—Taro. How? She had no clue. He was handsome, with shimmering black hair and thoughtful almond eyes. She'd like to meet him in person, but these waking images of him were shaking her up.

Cheska tried to shrug off the incident with the bookshelf. Then it had happened again a day later, and she knew she was cursed—strange abilities, visions of a person she'd never met? The Confab warned against such things. They told stories of the Skads, demons who could possess a person's body. The possession, they said, would manifest as strange abilities and behaviors, often with the possessed withdrawing from social situations. Cheska knew this all too well.

Since Cheska knew that she was different, by law, she was supposed to turn herself in to the nearest member of the Confab. Their local Vox was called Castus. Cheska knew him, but didn't like him at all. He was a creepy man with a tight pale face and wild eyes. They had red hair in common, but otherwise he might have been a different species.

No, she wouldn't be turning herself into Vox Castus —that would be a death sentence. The Covenant tolerated no deviations to their rigid genetic template. She would have to get this under control, hide it. What other choice did she have?

She'd learned that by focusing, she could eliminate accidental episodes. Conversely, she could now cause them to happen; which she did very carefully, and only when she was alone. This new ability might have been a wondrous gift, but not for a citizen of the Covenant. The Savior's Covenant had delivered mankind from its own folly—every Artaldean had the genetic memories of the apocalypse hard coded into their genome.

The Artaldean people had all but annihilated each other and their home-world. The Savior had come from afar, offering sanctuary to a select group, and a second chance to prosper. In exchange for that protection, each Artaldean would be born with the genetic memory of that apocalypse—in intense and disturbing detail. It was an Artaldean's most powerful and sensory rich memory. It had been a time of fire and death; a time of war and visceral horror. Brother killed brother, ate of other men's flesh, took their own sisters and daughter to wife.

Great cities had been reduced to smoking rubble while the planet lay cooling under a blanket of ash. Artaldeans were on the verge of extinction; then, the Savior had come, offering peace and harmony, health and happiness: The Covenant. The Savior had rescued them. His children were hence known as the Artaldeans. What name they had before that, none knew.

Thereafter, the only danger to the Artaldeans were the skads — demons who strove to return them to savagery; these fiends, the Savior warned about, and the Voces of the Confab preached against. They were the singular evil left in the Verse.

The terrifying realization for Cheska, was that she might become one of these demons.

***

"Hey there, Marmalade!" came her friend's voice.

Cheska turned to give Azara a scowl. "Why must you call me everything but Cheska?"

"Because it's cute? You're cute?" Azara shrugged and flashed a toothy smile.

They both laughed and snatched a quick hug.

"C'mon, let's get a seat before they lock us out," Cheska said.

The orientation room was much as Cheska expected, filled with a crowd of over a hundred people her age. All kids on what she and Azara called "adult row". As if they were being sentenced to adulthood for crimes previously committed. It was the popular joke for fifteen-year-olds.

They grabbed seats near other kids—some they knew well, others only in passing.

Vox Castus took the stage and set his hands on the lectern. Azara turned to her and rolled her eyes. "Here we go."

Castus was famous for his long windedness. He never had anything interesting to say, he just repeated the Confab's party line—pride in the candidates, thanking this person and that, blah blah blah, ad nauseum.

The obligatory clapping ensued. in which, Cheska pretended to participate.

"Thank you, citizens!" Vox Castus said. "It warms my heart to see so many bright faces in the crowd. You are the future of the Covenant." He nodded, as if he'd said something truly profound.

Azara glanced over to Cheska and rolled her eyes. Cheska suppressed a giggle. Azara was irreverent, but a hoot to hang out with. Cheska tried to stay out of trouble, though Azara was famous for squeezing them into that tight spot between right and wrong. Which was why Cheska's parents had never been enthusiastic about her choice of best friend. Too bad. She couldn't choose her family, but she could choose her friends, and she was determined to exercise that small freedom.

"Please allow me to introduce our first speaker," Vox Castus continued, "a noted engineer, and the gravitics prime on *Ghimorphos*, Dr. Madchen Foehner." He made a clapping motion at the crowd and applause ensued.

Now Cheska applauded for real. She admired Dr. Foehner's work, and was excited to be working in her department. Gravitics was one of the key technologies in Artaldean terraforming work. It was used to deflect ice and mineral-rich asteroids and comets to planets under terraforming. All that had been done decades ago for Krijese, but *Ghimorphos's* gravitic technology was still used to fine tune plate tectonics, and do other very heavy lifting.

As Dr. Foehner walked onto the stage, Cheska was surprised to see a welcoming, warm face, lit up with a seemingly genuine smile. She'd expected someone with a much sterner visage. That was even more promising. Dr. Foehner looked be in her mid-30's. She had chestnut hair tied back in a neat bun at the nape of her neck. She wore a navy-blue engineering jumpsuit with gold epaulettes and the rank insignia of Prime. She carried herself well. Cheska imagined herself as Dr. Foehner on the stage. Yep, that's who—what—she wanted to be. There was her future in blue and gold.

"Thank you, candidates. I appreciate the warm welcome." Her smile warmed Cheska, erasing all the stress of recent events. "You might be surprised at how few bodies of candidates really want to hear another dry speech from some old engineer like me." A few laughs rippled through the crowd. "So, I'll do you a favor … I won't give you a dull, dry, boring speech." She leaned onto the lectern, slumping casually. "Instead, let me tell you about how amazing it is to be a part of this mission. I'll let the folks after me tell you all about living quarters, weekend passes, and all that minutiae. That's not what gets me out of my quarters in the morning." An image of a rusty, dirty planet filled a screen behind Dr. Foehner. It had to be twenty-meters high.

"I have to be honest," Dr. Foehner continued, "I consider myself more an artist than an engineer." Suddenly, the dead looking world was replaced by one with greens and blues, seas and forests. "This is my canvas." She turned back to marvel at the image, shaking her head. "Look at that … I created that." She turned back to the audience. "We created that. Myself, your parents, and grandparents. And you get to complete it." She put her hands out wide and grinned like a little girl. "I might not see Krijese populated, but that dream is what gets me up in the morning." She paused for a moment. "In the years to come, there will be lots of hard, long days. There may be days that you wish you'd never tested well for this job or that job." She paused again, then pointed back to the living world on screen. "But remember this. Remember what you're building."

Cheska was tingling all over. She'd never felt this inspired. She wanted to leap out of her seat and fly to the planet right now! By the Savior, she'd finish it herself! She could do anything!

What she hadn't meant to do, was to stop time.

***

The entire auditorium was frozen. At first Cheska thought she'd just blanked out. But when she turned her head and looked around, not a person was moving or making a sound. She knew she was in trouble.

Previously, her episodes had manifested in bursts of physical speed. If she wasn't moving, nobody would notice, right? When none moved after a few seconds Cheska's stomach churned, cold creeping down her limbs. Had she killed them all? Great Savior!

She leaped out of her seat, noting that Azara was frozen mid-word, leaned in and about to say something to her. Cheska picked her way up the aisle to the rear of the auditorium and the exit.

Jak burst in through the doors, eyes wide. "What happened?"

Skads! His sudden outburst after the deathly quiet was even more alarming. What could she say? She shook her head dumbly, not even muttering a sound.

"You're a timebender," Jak said with awe. 'We've been waiting for you." Jak grabbed her by the arm and tugged her through the exit. "We need to get out of here! Now!"

Cheska felt a burst of adrenaline coursing through her veins. A voice erupted from behind her—it was Dr. Foehner, standing in the doorway, mouth agape.

"Whaaaa- Waa-" she was trying to speak, but looked drugged, sedated. She stumbled through the exit, the door closing behind her.

"No time, m'am. You'll have to come with us."

Jak dragged the two women down the passageways in a very controlled fashion. Cheska imagined this is how he might have to arrest someone. Wait, was she under arrest? She just noticed that he was in his civilian clothes and unarmed. Surely he'd have brought a weapon to arrest her?

"That was very close, young lady," Jak chided.

"It's not what you think!" Cheska pleaded. Her stomach suddenly roiled. "I'm gonna be sick!" She pulled back on his grip, dry-heaving.

Jak glared at her. "No time! Pull it together. Understand me?"

Cheska had never seen a look of such intensity on Jak's face, not in the two years they'd known each other. He'd been a bastion of warmth and kindness, of gentle support.

"I- " she began.

Dr. Foehner seemed to be in a trance, walking in perfect compliance, but saying nothing.

Jak stopped suddenly, his features softening as he

looked at Cheska. "It's ok, kiddo. I know what to do. Didn't I tell you I'd always look out for you?"

She nodded.

He returned the nod solemnly. "Right. And a Watcher always keeps his promise." He forced a small smile.

That helped, but Cheska still felt like vomiting.

"C'mon," Jak said, "I have a lot to explain."

Codename Raven

AS THEY NEARED CHESKA'S QUARTERS, another Watcher rounded the corner. Cheska shuddered.

The Watcher put up a hand to wave to Jak. But it was too late—Cheska panicked. Without meaning too, she sped up and flashed past him, while both Jak and this second Watcher stood frozen. She inhaled sharply as time resumed its normal flow.

A look of horror painted the Watcher's face. "Blessed Savior! Captain! She's Abhuman!" He drew his sidearm in a flash, training it on Cheska's body.

Without thinking, Cheska tried to stop him. Her instinct was to disarm him, but when she sped up, she slammed right into him, knocking the pistol out of his hand. She still had some momentum and dove for the pistol. She trained the pistol on him, the weapon shaking.

The Watcher held out his hands in a calming gesture. "Listen to me, young lady. I know you're scared. But we can get you help. Let me call Vox Castus and we'll see about some treatment, ok?" He glanced over to Jak, probably wondering why his Captain didn't tackle her.

Jak sighed. "There's no other choice," he said to Cheska.

She turned to see his face, trying to make sense of what she'd just heard. Had he just told her to kill this Watcher? One of his own men?

Dr. Foehner's eyes went as wide as comms dishes, but still she stood in mute silence.

Jak shook his head ruefully. "It's gotta be done, kiddo."

"Captain! What in the Core?" The Watcher cursed.

"Do it," Jak said evenly.

The Watcher lunged at Cheska. She recoiled. Her hand squeezed reflexively, triggering a shrill burst of plasma and an accompanying flare of purple. She would never forget the look on the man's face. Or the sound, or the smell of his burnt flesh … of the man she had murdered.

The plasma pistol clattered to the floor and Cheska slumped to her knees.

Jak grabbed her arm again, yanking her to her feet. "No time. You did what you had to do, you survived."

"No!" Cheska screamed, twisting out of Jak's grip with enhanced speed.

"Hold up, kid," Jak said. "I'll get you out of this, ok?

You trust me?"

She'd just noticed she was gasping for air—panic. She tried to get her breathing under control.

Jak spoke with a calm, soothing voice. "We don't have time to stand here. But I *will* get you out of this. I promise you." He proffered a hand.

She took it. He nodded, smiling.

"Where?" she managed to whisper.

"Off the *Ghimorphos*. We won't be coming back."

***

Still below street level, they travelled down the *Ghimorphos's* wide octagonal passageways. Since it was orientation day, many of the teenagers and adults were occupied with extra duties, making for very few onlookers who might ask questions.

Jak still held onto Dr. Foehner who remained as docile as a napping baby, but had released his grip on Cheska. She no longer needed encouragement to run. She knew full well what waited for her if she stayed on *Ghimorphos*—a swift trip to the Core and eternal suffering. She shuddered as she recalled stories of the place. The Core was the place where the damned went. Abhumans, deviants, possessed—whatever they were called—they all went to the Core; none returned. She'd known a couple of people over the years who'd been sent. Was she truly one of them? Tears welled up in her eyes. She wiped them away angrily. She had to be stronger than that right now.

"My mother?" Cheska asked Jak.

He shook his head grimly.

Of course. She'd never see her again. Or Azara.

Cheska stopped abruptly. "I can't run. I- this has to be some mistake. No. This can't be happening." She squeezed her eyes shut and clenched her fists.

Jak spun on her. "Damnit, girl! Do. You. Want. To. Die?"

She shook her head weakly.

"Then move your ass!" Jak grabbed her arm again and yanked her forward, his other hand firmly clamped onto Dr. Foehner's arm.

As they ran, Jak tapped his wrist-comm. "Code name Raven. I need help with an extraction."

Codename Raven? Cheska thought.

***

They arrived at Ngome City's docking-hub without incident.

A tech in soiled yellow coveralls met them at an enormous, ten-meter wide door. He nodded to Jak. "The *Ghimorphos's* sensors will be going into thirty-minute diagnostic test mode. That should give you time to get below cloud cover and slip away." He handed a small package to Jak.

"Thank you," Jak said.

"Good luck, Raven," the man said as he keyed in a code to the security panel.

Jak nodded. The door hissed as it rose into the ceiling. The acrid smell of chemicals and overly dry air, assaulted Cheska's nose. The docking-hub hangar was huge—at least one-hundred meters across. A squat looking supply shuttle sat on the pad, whining engines spooling up for launch. Jak motioned for her to follow.

He jogged to the shuttle and rapped on the hatch,

peering through the tiny porthole above it. They waited for a moment and a section of the hatch faded from opaque to translucent. A young man with an annoyed expression stared out at them.

"What?" Came a voice over the external speaker.

Jak produced his badge. "Security inspection."

"Skads, Captain! We're already behind schedule," the man complained. The hatch irised open. "Can you make it quick?"

"I'll do the best I can," Jak said.

"Uniform dirty?" the young man asked.

"What?" Jak asked.

The young man motioned to Jak's civilian garb.

"Oh, yeah, random inspection on the gravitics systems. I got told five minutes ago, no time to change. I just do what they tell me," Jak said, tilting his head to Dr. Foehner.

"I hear that," Carver said—Cheska could see his name tag now. "Trainee?" he asked, motioning to Cheska.

"Yeah, my new apprentice," Jak said, clapping a hand on Cheska's shoulder.

When Carver turned to Cheska, she offered him a toothy grin. He gave her a slow, very impressed nod. "Lucky girl. Working under the Captain of the Watchers? Your parents must know people, huh?"

Cheska shrugged.

When Carver noticed Dr. Foehner's epaulettes and insignia, he realized who she was. "We've never had the Gravitics Prime do a spot check. I hope the shuttle's ok?"

"I'm sure it's fine," Jak said. "The Doc is a cautious lady. Right Doc?" He tugged her arm but she stared blankly at him. Jak rolled his eyes to Carver and shrugged.

Cheska wasn't sure what Jak's plan was, but as the hatch hissed closed behind her, she prayed to the Savior that they wouldn't have to kill anyone else.

***

There were only four crew aboard the shuttle; standard for a cargo run to re-supply the terraforming teams. Jak subdued each of the crew in moments—Watchers were handpicked for their size and unflappability. Their mere presence projected an effective deterrent against most unruly behavior.

Jak went to the aft cargo compartment to tie up and secure the crew. When he returned he said, "Let's get buckled up. I'm hoping we can launch without too much interference, but I've never hi-jacked a shuttle before." He turned to smile at Cheska. "Never know, right? Could be smooth sailing."

He helped Dr. Foehner to a passenger bench and buckled her in before taking the pilot's seat. Cheska slid in beside him at the co-pilot's station and fastened her four-point harness.

"*What are we going to do with her?*" Cheska whispered. She was really hoping his answer didn't involve manslaughter.

"We'll let her go once we get down safely. I didn't want her warning anyone on the ship about you."

Thank the Savior. She didn't think her safety was worth even one life, let alone two. "Thank you, by the way."

"For what?" Jak asked.

"For saving my life."

He shared a half smile with her. "We're not there yet, kiddo. And hey, what are friends for?"

Cheska could not imagine Azara saving her from the Core. Azara was pretty devout. Cheska was fairly certain Azara would have turned her in to Vox Castus —best friends be damned!

She watched Jak work at the holographic controls for a moment and the shuttle began to rise off the pad. She noticed the force-field flicker as the outer doors slid open. The shuttle accelerated smoothly out into the abyss of space.

The front of the shuttle disappeared, replaced by a projection of the outside world in vivid detail. To the shuttle's pilots, it was like driving a glass bubble. Though, what felt like an expansive window was actually a structurally reinforced bulkhead. The illusion was very convincing.

"Nothing to it," Jak said, as the shuttle slipped away from the *Ghimorphos*.

Cheska marveled at the view. For the first time in her life she was seeing the *Ghimorphos* from the outside. Despite the chaos and horrors of the day, Cheska felt a rush of wonder. It was breathtaking! Nine domed habitats perched on the outside of the central sphere; like petals on a flower. From their trajectory, she could make out three of the nine. Hab 6, which the locals called Al'Qafis, glittered in shades of blue and silver; it was dedicated to water reclamation and air purification.

Hab 7, Insparra, looked solid in stoney grays and whites. It's buildings were the training grounds for the *Ghimorphos's* legal and spiritual experts. Brilliant shades of green dominated Hab 8. Better known as Khola, it was one of several habitats devoted to agriculture.

As quickly as the joy had warmed her … it cooled. She realized she would never see home again. She choked back more tears.

"You ok?" Jak asked.

"*Why wouldn't I be?*" She whispered, sniffling.

"If you want to talk about it … we have a three hour flight."

"Flight to where exactly?"

"To a safe place." Jak said.

"Why is this happening to me? I never had one heretical thought in my sixteen years. I've always done what was expected of me." She shook her head. "I don't get it."

"It's not what you did, Cheska, it's who—or rather, what, you are."

"And *what* am I exactly? Artaldean, last time I checked. Sixteen-years-old."

"Happy birthday?" he offered.

The whole situation was so completely absurd she chuckled. "Thanks. Get me anything nice?"

"I did." He gestured around the cockpit. "A shuttle!" Jak grinned.

Cheska tried to smile.

They flew in silence for a while, the rusty-blue mottled surface of Krijese looming ever larger as they descended to the surface.

"I've been having dreams lately," Cheska said.

Jak nodded. "Uh huh."

"About a boy."

"Oh. I had those too when I was your age. About girls- but I imagine they were the same sort."

"No!" She scowled at Jak. "Not like that! I dreamt I was on Krijese, but it was green in places. And the dreams were the most vivid I've ever had. And then this boy appeared. Taro."

Jak turned and met her eyes with a serious look.

"Sometimes they happen when I'm asleep, but mostly when I'm wide awake. And we talk, and I remember everything—so does he, because we continue the conversations in the next dream."

Jak looked very worried, which unnerved Cheska. "What is it?"

He shook his head slowly. "Where the Core do I begin? Firstly, you are not possessed. You are not a deviant. You're what they call Abhuman."

"Abhuman? I thought you said I was a timebender?"

He nodded. "You're both."

"Who are they?"

"Oh boy. You're not going to like this part."

"Am I supposed to be liking any of this? I found out I'm a timebender- Abhuman- whatever. I murdered a Watcher, stole a shuttle, and am now a fleeing criminal. Did I miss anything?"

Jak nodded. "Yeah, you did."

Cheska looked at him with horror and disbelief. "You're kidding me, right?"

"Nope. Ever heard of the Prophecy of the Comps?"

He didn't wait for her to answer. "Probably not. So, back to the Abhuman part. Being Abhuman is not a bad thing—bear with me. When the Covenant deems a person a deviant, or possessed, that individual is usually Abhuman—their term—which means away from human. Abhumans have extraordinary gifts; some, very powerful, some, rather minor. Your gift- "

"My curse." Cheska interrupted.

"Your *gifts*," Jak repeated patiently, "are very powerful."

Cheska was overwhelmed. She could not process all this right now. She shook it off and turned to look over her shoulder at the Doctor. "You think Dr. Foehner is ok?"

Jak shook his head. "In shock maybe? It's not everyday you come face to face with a deviant." He winked at Cheska.

She scowled. "Hey now! I thought I was Abhuman?"

Jak shook his head. "Nothing wrong with you at all, kiddo. Don't believe it for a second. It's a system designed to keep us afraid and turning on each other. That way we don't see the real threat, the real evil."

"What is the real evil?"

"That's a very long story. Let's get you safe, then I'll tell you what I know. My friends will tell you more."

"What friends?"

Jak sighed. "Would you let me focus on piloting the shuttle?"

"I thought these things basically flew themselves?"

"I can see I'm not going to win this argument, am-"

Krboom!

An explosion rocked the shuttle, fire flashed on the view-screen.

The shuttle bucked and Jak's eyes went wide, as did Cheska's. He glanced at her with a look of confusion.

A klaxon sound hit them like a bucket of cold water.

Brrng Brrng Brrng Brrng

She recoiled, holding up her hands. "I didn't do anything!"

The holographic console in front of them lit up like a peacock's tail, but one flashing red indicator dominated the scene. "We've lost attitude control."

"What happened?" Cheska asked.

"Hold tight, landing is not going to be pretty."

The shuttle's nose banked over and down, and began screaming toward the surface in a violent corkscrew. Cheska's head felt crushed by the oppressive centripetal force as the shuttle performed its death-spiral. What was more concerning, was that Jak looked panicked. She'd hoped he could fix this. If he looked scared … they were in serious trouble.

Cheska strained to look out the tiny porthole above the hatch as Jak struggled in vain with the controls. She caught a flash in her peripheral vision. Jak slumped forward in his seat, his head lolling. One of the crew had clambered forward and held a length of piping in his hand. The same piping he'd just smacked Jak in the head with!

Cheska was horrified as the crewman began unbuckling Jak from his harness. He'd somehow escaped confinement and, had made his way forward while the shuttle was spinning.

"Don't!" she shouted.

The man glared at her.

Cheska did the only thing she could, she kicked at him. He lost his grip and went careening into the side of the shuttle, stuck by the increasing g-force.

The ground was getting much larger, much faster. Cheska reached over and tried to fasten up the two buckles of Jak's harness, which now flapped with the centripetal force of the spinning shuttle. She couldn't quite reach. And she dare not unbuckle herself. Her heart hammered in her chest.

The crewman cursed at her as he tried to climb back toward the cockpit flight controls, hand over hand. She glanced back out the window and didn't think the crewman would have time to get to her anyway. They were coming in too fast. They'd crater into the surface by the time he got close.

She prayed to the Savior, as that had always been a comfort.

He didn't answer.

Cheska's entire body burned with the anticipation.

She squinted, her face puckering.

She braced for impact.

And screamed!

***

Cheska's mind prepared for pain and death; neither came. She realized she was holding her breath and sucked in a lungful of air. She opened her eyes, expecting to see the afterlife. Instead, she saw the shuttle cockpit. And it wasn't spinning. In fact, nothing moved.

She turned back to see the crewman, his face frozen

in a rictus of hatred, still clawing his way toward the pilot's chair. But he was frozen. So was Jak. So was Dr. Foehner. So was the shuttle! It was frozen on a forty five-degree angle. She glanced out the tiny window and saw the ground clearly—maybe five meters away.

Cheska realized what was happening, or thought she did. She unbuckled her harness and moved toward Jak. She unfastened his last two buckles and dragged him out of the pilot's seat. Thank the Savior the hatch was below them, and not above. As it was, she just pushed Jak toward the hatch and he slid down the forty-five degree incline.

She let go of his seat and piled down on top of Jak. Dr. Foehner's seat was directly beside the hatch, so Cheska only had to unbuckle her. Now Dr. Foehner was piled limp on top of Jak.

Cheska spied a rack of breathers which the crew would have had to use—the atmospheric transformation of Krijese was still incomplete. She'd been told the atmosphere was breathable for a couple of hours, but any longer and they'd be in trouble. She grabbed four—one for a spare, then looked to the two slumped bodies on the hatch.

"I'm really sorry about this," Cheska said, then grabbed a hand rail and slapped the hatch-open release. When it irised open, Jak and Dr. Foehner fell into a pile on the ochre mud below. Cheska's legs dangled out of the hatch and she let go of the hand rail, falling onto Jak and Dr. Foehner.

"Damn it!" Her knee smarted, but she didn't have time to worry about it. She slapped Jak hard across the face, waking him, sort of. He still looked dazed. "Follow me! Help with Dr. Foehner if you can!" She put the breather in her mouth then popped one onto each of them, stowing the fourth on her belt.

Jak shook his head, clearly dazed, but he began crawling in the direction Cheska had indicated.

She winced as she put weight on her left knee, but grabbed Dr. Foehner under the shoulders and began to drag her away from the shuttle, which was still suspended, frozen in mid flight—maybe seven meters away now. She knew her time manipulation didn't last long—she might only have seconds to get Dr. Foehner away from the point of impact. Jak was trying to stand, but only managed a crawl. Thank the Savior he could crawl because she didn't think she could have dragged him.

Cheska screamed as she thrust up with her thighs, digging her heels into the soft cloying ground and dragging Dr. Foehner's limp form, inch, by agonizing inch. Cheska felt a tingling in her brain and knew her hold on the shuttle was coming to an end. Please, not yet!

Her brain processed a flash of motion before she was thrown off her feet. Her vision faded to black.

***

Cheska's head seared like an inferno as vision returned. The pain was so overwhelming, she gasped. A dark skinned face came into view—Jak.

"You ok, kiddo?" he asked.

"Great Savior! You tell me. I feel like- " She winced as she tried to move, realizing her entire body ached. "I fell like I've been in a shuttle crash." She tried to smile.

"Glad to see your sense of humor isn't broke. I checked you over. You might have some cracked ribs, but you've got no broken bones that I can tell. A few cuts and bruises is all."

Pain flashed like lightning, thundering in her brain. "I feel like I've been to the Core and back."

"Uh huh."

Cheska realized Jak looked untouched by the crash. "I dropped you five or more meters unconscious. How are you doing?"

"Don't you worry about me. Watchers are tough. We have to be." He gave Cheska his famous ear-to-ear smile that warmed her soul every time she saw it. She loved Jak. She began to cry.

"What's wrong? Pain?" he asked.

"No," she managed between sniffs. "I'm just- " She sniffed again. "I'm just glad you're here with me. You're all I have left, Jak."

"Hey now, listen … don't worry about all that now, ok? We've got to get ourselves away from this crash site."

She nodded, wiping her eyes.

"You saved my life you know," Jak stated solemnly.

"I guess we're even then, huh?"

"Not quite."

"What do you mean?" Cheska asked.

"You busted up that nice shuttle I got you for your birthday."

Jak helped her up, then wiped tears from her cheek with his big thumb. "I got your back, kiddo. Don't you ever forget that."

Cheska nodded. She wouldn't.

The shuttle had cratered into the soft red mud, and she guessed that's what had knocked her out. There had been no explosion after the initial one that had damaged the shuttle. Jak checked the wreckage to see if there were survivors—there weren't any; very little remained of the four crewmen.

Jak salvaged a plasteel-spar from the shuttle wreckage which he fashioned into a crude crutch for Cheska. It wasn't comfortable to use, but at least she could hobble along now.

"No plasma-rifle?" Cheska asked.

"Buried or burnt up, I imagine."

"And yes, I'm fine too. Thanks for asking," Dr. Foehner said with a scowl, hands on her hips. She was talking now, and alert. "Where the Core am I?"

Jak turned to Cheska and shrugged, as if to say, 'where do we start?'

SOJOURN

DELFINA CIFUENTES ROLLED OUT OF bed, a sheet draped around her naked body, clinging to patches of sweat. She peered back over her shoulder to see Gaios stirring. What the hell was she doing? She knew having a relationship with someone under her command was a bad idea, but since everyone in Sanctuary was under her command, then who? Besides, she'd been lonely.

Running the Aoratos was a solitary post by nature—she'd known that when she took the job. She'd also known what was at stake, and her needs shouldn't ever factor into it. Not one little bit. Damned regret. She didn't have time to waste on it. This would be the last time with the good Doctor. He wouldn't like it, but too bad for him.

She let the sheet slip to the floor as she stepped into the shower stall. She turned on the water and let it beat down on her skin, cleansing her body, if not her sins. Regret always brought her thoughts back to *him*. The one she'd lost so many years ago. Twelve years, three months and five days. Yes, she remembered. You never forgot your first true love. Never.

The door to the stall opened and she saw Gaios's grinning face.

"Want some company?" he said smoothly.

"No." She pushed him back and closed the semi-translucent stall door.

Gaios held his hands up in a defeated gesture. "Can I get you some coffee?" He offered.

"No." She snapped, then softened. It wasn't his fault she felt guilty. She didn't need to be a bitch. But it did make it easier. "I'll get some when I get to my office."

"Ok. See you later?" he asked hopefully.

She shrugged noncommittally.

He took the hint and waved, moving off to get dressed.

Delfina stayed under the water until she heard Gaios leave her quarters.

Once she was dressed in her duty coveralls, she stepped to her dresser mirror. She picked up a small circular pendant on a chain. On the thumb-sized pendant a symbol like three pieces of pie around a small circle was inscribed—the symbol of the Savior's Covenant. She no longer believed in such things, but he had given it to her all those years ago. She wore it always. The only time she took it off was when she was with Gaios. She felt not to do so would be an insult to him. She wanted a reminder of him near her always, except when other needs intruded for a few moments here and there.

She placed a hand reverently over the pendant and started into the mirror. Was she still the beautiful girl he had paired with? She smiled at that thought. Maybe. She dragged a brush through her long black tresses.

She heard the chirping of her wristcom from beneath a pile of towels and retrieved it. "Yes?"

"M'am, we have a surface contact."

***

Dr. Foehner seemed to have completely recovered from her shock or temporary coma, or whatever had been wrong her. Now she was just pissed. The warm and friendly woman Cheska remembered from the auditorium was gone.

"This is kidnapping, Captain. You know that?" Dr. Foehner asked with a stern look on her face.

"Yes m'am." Jak said humbly.

"They'll send you to the Core for this. You know that too?"

"Yes, m'am."

"Don't m'am me, you're older than I am!"

"Yes, m'am."

Dr. Foehner shook her head with frustration. "Well, I suppose we'll just wait here for rescue." She looked around, seeming to be searching for a suitable place to sit. There were none. Nothing but a flat expanse of red mud and dirt, and mountains off into the distance to either side.

"No, m'am. We can't do that. We have to leave."

"No, we most certainly are not," Dr. Foehner said.

"Dr. Foehner," Cheska said, with as sweet a tone as she could muster, "please, come with us. I don't think it's safe for you to be alone here."

"What are you doing with this … *rebel*? You're a bright young woman. I reviewed your placement test scores, Ms. Bellamy, you topped the list this year. Did you know that? I personally requested you be assigned to my gravitics division."

Cheska knew she'd done well by virtue of her posting, but she didn't know what her scores were. To avoid ill will between students, such numbers were rarely shared publicly. Of course, if you knew the right people, anything was possible. And to know that Dr. Foehner had requested her for the gravitics posting— that was bittersweet.

She shook her head.

"Let's go, kiddo. We've got at least two days of hard trekking ahead of us." Jak began walking away.

Cheska stared at Dr. Foehner pleadingly, but the Gravitics Prime was a determined woman. Cheska imagined she was used to getting her way, as a confident and intelligent woman should. Cheska turned and took a step.

"Damn you both," Dr. Foehner muttered, then followed.

Cheska smiled but didn't turn back.

***

As Thorantis began to set over the distant mountains, Cheska imagined it was a glowing red eye being devoured by a jagged set of fangs.

Krijese was the second of seven planets in the Thorantis system, a solitary red-dwarf star. There were very few soft curves on what Cheska could see of the planet; that would take thousands of years of physical and biochemical weathering. Now Krijese had an unforgiving look to it. It was all sharp lines and pointy bits.

Cheska marveled at the redness of the place. They stood under a grey and crimson sky, clouds lit by the setting red dwarf, and they trod upon rusty soil. They'd have to invent new names for the different shades of red. She could only recall a handful—they'd need a lot more.

The shuttle had crashed in a valley between two new mountain ranges, which seemed to run parallel to each other off into the distance. At the end of the rocky corridor, a titanic mountain loomed over them. It was the tallest thing Cheska had ever seen.

The expanse of rusty mud was only broken by sporadic pockets of blue—new ground water she assumed—and white, where the water had frozen. For the last few decades they'd been re-vectoring icy comets and meteorites, crashing them into the surface, adding water, but also throwing billions of cubic tons of dust up into the atmosphere. It had taken years for much it to settle down and the planet had gone into a bit of an ice age. Now it was a muddy mess.

The current project, which was Dr. Foehner's area of expertise, was gravitic-tectonic manipulation. The terraforming teams used the ultra powerful tractor beams on the *Ghimorphos* to push and pull the tectonic plates into optimal positions. They had also used tractor beams to create a crude moon.

The three survivors only managed 5 km progress on the first day. Given that they'd crashed close to sunset, the terrain was slick and muddy, and with Cheska's ankle injury, it was about half what Jak had hoped for.

It could have been much worse—crashing 72 km from their destination was a blessing. Had the explosion happened at a much higher altitude, they could have come down a thousand kilometers away. Maybe the Savior had been looking out for Cheska?

That first night was cold. They had no tools or fuel to start a fire. Jak and Cheska snuggled up together for heat, but Dr. Foehner was having none of that—shared body heat be damned. The three survivors lay huddled up under the shelter of a rock ledge surrounded by few boulders. At least they were out of the wind.

"So," Dr. Foehner said, "you still haven't answered my question, Cheska. Why are you consorting with this criminal?"

How did she answer that? Technically, she and Jak were both criminals now. How much could, or should, she tell Dr. Foehner? She decided it didn't really matter. Cheska was never going home, and whatever she told Dr. Foehner was therefore irrelevant. But it might pass the time to talk.

"He's not a criminal, Dr. Foehner, I am."

Dr. Foehner narrowed her eyes.

Cheska continued, "I'm a deviant, an Abhuman."

Dr. Foehner's eyes now went wide. "What? Are you

sure? My dear, that is quite a leap."

Cheska nodded.

Jak gave Cheska a little squeeze as they snuggled for warmth.

"How do you know you're an Abhuman?" Dr. Foehner asked.

"I can freeze time, I'm pretty sure that's not normal."

Eyebrows raised, the Doctor seemed to consider that. "No. I suppose it isn't. Since we're getting to know each other, you might as well call me Madchen." Cheska nodded. "You know, Cheska, you could have talked to someone. The Confab could have gotten you treatment."

"That's crap!" Cheska blurted out. "I saw what they did to Yichang three years ago. Straight to the Core. And for what? For saving my mother's life? I could understand if these Abhumans started murdering people, but I've never heard of that happening. Only the Confab murders people."

Dr. Foehner shook her head. "That's just not true."

"Of course it is, m'am," Jak said. "I'm Captain of the Watchers. I've delivered half a dozen people to trial at the Confab. No deviant has ever gone for treatment. They go one place—the Core."

***

Being stranded on the planet had shattered Cheska's illusion of the life she had imagined having here: fantasies in cerulean blue and emerald green, of birds flying and animals crawling, of children playing and lovers laughing. Krijese reminded her of what of the Core might be like—a place suffering and eternal torture. She'd struggled with that concept as a younger child; the fact that a benevolent being, such as the Savior, needed such a horrific place to punish people. Surely there had to be a more Artaldean way? But then vivid memories of the Apocalypse coursed through her brain, cementing the need for the Savior, and justifying the terror of the Core as a preventative measure. The Artaldeans might very well destroy themselves again if not for these safeguards. They were for the best, she decided.

The second day the ground firmed up, which was good news. The bad news was that it was frozen. That meant another cold night ahead, and at their current pace, and assuming the terrain didn't get worse, it was going to be another four days. All three of them wore clothing manufactured from bionan fabric, which provided a modest range of climatic protection. A wearer could be comfortable from -5 °C to 30 °C. Anything above or below that, would overload the suit's capacity to regulate.

They drank from frozen over pools of cometary ice water, which were plentiful enough, but hunger began to plague Cheska on the second day. She assumed Jak and Dr. Foehner were also hungry, but neither complained.

Mid-afternoon on the third day Jak's hand darted up with his fist clenched—his signal for them to stop and freeze in place; he'd taught them a basic vocabulary of hand signals the Watchers used. He gave them a second signal to take cover, though there wasn't much to hide behind. They were still in a wide valley between two mountain ranges, the terrain mostly flat.

Cheska could see some kind of rock formation, that might have been a hill. That's what she thought had gotten Jak's attention. She and Dr. Foehner dutifully lay on their stomachs. While they lay prone, Jak crept forward. He walked a few hundred meters up the hill and seemed to crest it. He stood still for a long while, then motioned for them to follow.

When Cheska and Dr. Foehner scrambled up the incline and stood beside Jak, they were breathless—but not from exertion.

A massive crater spread out before the small hill. None of it had been visible from the other side. It stretched out for kilometers.

"This can't be," Dr. Foehner whispered.

"Damn," Jak mumbled.

Cheska didn't have words to describe the horror of the scene below.

***

The crater wasn't what had them speechless and stunned—it was the city. More accurately, the battered and broken ruins of a city. Dr. Foehner slumped down and sat in the dirt. She sat shaking her head.

Jak wandered down into the crater and began looking through some of the ruins.

"There were people here once?" Cheska asked. There shouldn't have been. Even if there were ruins, she understood that the Covenant passed over such worlds in case there were any archaeological ruins of note.

"Not once ... recently," Dr. Foehner said.

"What? How recently?" Cheska asked, taking a seat beside her.

"You're a smart young woman, Cheska. What do you see?" Dr. Foehner said.

Cheska ran her eyes over the crater, back and forth—buildings, some quite tall judging by the length of the remains. She didn't see any weathering on the buildings, nor any signs of subtle decay. There were great rents in the earth, and in a few cases she spotted lines of magma —which warmed the area to a comfortable degree. She felt suddenly queasy as the sight of the ruins evoked embedded memory of the Apocalypse for the second time in two days—each time overloading the senses.

"It was a cataclysm," Cheska said.

Dr. Foehner nodded and pointed higher up on the crater wall. "See there?"

She spied ice. Cheska nodded.

"We did this. Those look like remnants of a comet, or icy meteorite that we directed planet-side."

"But I thought- " Cheska began.

"So did I," Dr. Foehner said. "And I saw planetary surveys. There were no cities here. At least none on the data I was provided by the survey teams."

"Why would they have lied about that? It makes no sense," Cheska asked.

"No. It doesn't," Dr. Foehner said.

They sat in silence for a long time. The implications were monstrous. The *Ghimorphos* had been on station over Krijese for over a century. Most building materials would have shown some signs of weathering had they been ancient. Buildings less than a century destroyed however, would look pretty much as Cheska saw lying shattered before her.

Had anyone lived here recently? Maybe there had been some atmospheric crisis and an evacuation? There had to be a million reasons why the Covenant would have proceeded with terraforming. But then why did Dr. Foehner not know about the ruins? If a decision had been made, and there was no harm, why not tell the gravitics Prime? She was a very senior engineer. Cheska may not have been worldly, but she was both intuitive and logical. This situation was anything but logical; sadly, intuition provided no answers.

Jak had been gone for what seemed like an hour and Cheska began to worry. Dr. Foehner hadn't spoken in long time, seemingly back in a fugue state like their encounter at the auditorium. Cheska stood up. "I'm going to find Jak. Are you coming?"

Dr. Foehner nodded and followed.

The crater was deep but the slope shallow enough, so they wandered down looking for Jak. Alternately shouting his name. They followed his footprints in the mud and dirt, but then the dirt gave way to a hard road surface. It astounded Cheska that anything of these buildings and roads remained after being hit by a comet or meteorite. With the mass required to form this size of crater, there should be nothing but dust, yet here they were; remnants of buildings, like toys that had been broken up and buried in sand.

It was when they found the first corpse that Cheska really knew the full measure of the atrocity committed here. It was a small humanoid. A child perhaps? Not an

Artaldean, but definitely a bipedal humanoid, with an elongated egg-shaped skull tapering at the back. The corpse was desiccated, but signs of blunt force trauma painted a horrific picture of the creature's end.

Cheska thought she should be crying, but her tears were long spent.

They found Jak kneeling beside the bodies of what had to have been a family. Two larger humanoids and three smaller ones, huddled together.

"I had no idea," Dr. Foehner said.

"I believe you, Doc," Jak said. "A lot of us have been deceived for a very long time." He stood and brushed the silt from his pants. "We're gonna fix that," he held Dr. Foehner's gaze and nodded. "Aren't we?"

She nodded solemnly.

Cheska believed she meant it.

Jak lay a hand on Dr. Foehner's shoulder. She closed her eyes as she lay a hand on top of his.

Cheska traced her fingers along an intricate design in what must be a piece of a building exterior. The design was a flowing spiral that branched off into wispy tendrils, intertwined and seeming to dance. "Beautiful," she whispered.

"Down!" Jak whispered loudly.

Cheska and Dr. Foehner dropped beside the remains of broken wall. Cheska glanced around, looking for whatever had spooked Jak.

Two bipedal creatures wearing full environment suits and armed with some kind of weapons seemed to be patrolling the streets. They were Artaldean sized, maybe bigger, but the helmets had elongated heads. They walked in a strange gate, their legs bending backward, where an Artaldean knees bent forward. The three survivors stayed silent a long while as the creatures passed by.

Cheska slithered up close to Jak. "Do you think there are more of them?"

He shook his head slowly. "Dunno, but we need to get out of this crater. It seems like they're hanging around the ruins of this city. Though I don't know why. Nothing here but the dead."

Jak motioned for them to move out quietly.

***

They saw no more of the humanoids but on the fourth day they spotted a cluster of atmospheric generators. The machines were designed to analyze the local atmosphere and continually tweak and fine tune the composition—sometimes producing nitrogen, other-times carbon dioxide, or whatever was needed.

After Jak made sure there were no techs manning the generators, Cheska and Dr. Foehner walked up to the structures.

There was a large hole in the side of the closest generator. Cheska lay a hand on a ragged piece of metal on the edge off the hole, noting a black residue. "Look at the charring."

"Looks like an explosion," Dr. Foehner said. She craned her head into the hole then turned back to Cheska. "Notice anything unusual about this?"

"Other than a hole in what should be a working atmo-generator?" She surveyed the damage again. Then it clicked. "The blast came from outside."

55

"Precisely. That was no industrial accident."

"Sabotage?" Jak asked.

"That's the most likely conclusion," Dr. Foehner said.

"Well, nothing we can do about it," Jak said. "Let's keep moving."

As they began to walk away from the atmospheric generators, Dr. Foehner stumbled, falling to her knees. Cheska trudged over to help her up. They were weak. All of them, though Jak didn't seem to show it. Four days without food. She'd never been hungry before, not really. She barely had the strength to put one foot in front of the other, and Jak set a relentless pace.

Cheska proffered a hand to Dr. Foehner. She put up a hand, staving off Cheska's aid. "Just give me a minute."

Jak, who had been in the lead, circled back to where Dr. Foehner had fallen. "You ok, Doc?"

"Think- so. Just so tired." Dr. Foehner looked up to Jak with a pleading in her eyes. Cheska felt it too. She wanted to lay down and sleep.

"We can go weeks without food you know. You'll live. I know it's unpleasant, but we have to keep moving," Jak said.

Dr. Foehner let out a weak laugh. "Weeks? Great Savior, I don't know if I'll last the day, Captain."

"You will. I promise," he said.

Cheska felt a tiny surge of hope. "A Watcher always keeps his promises, Dr. Foehner," Cheska said.

"Well, in that case …" Dr. Foehner held up a hand for Jak and Cheska each. They hoisted her back to her feet. "Lead on, Captain."

The entire fifth day they spent approaching the largest mountain they'd seen yet on Krijese. It seemed to have burst up alone at the end of the other two ranges, almost like a marker, or a great ochre sentinel. It soared twice as high as anything in the adjacent ranges. All day it loomed before them, as if watching them, taking the measure of them. In their famished and exhausted state it seemed to mock them. 'You dare approach me?' it might have been saying.

Cheska screamed as six creatures burst up from the ground in clouds of dust.

Jak threw an arm protectively in front Cheska.

The six humanoids wore heavy vac-suits and had weapons trained on them.

They'd appeared about a stone's throw in front of Cheska   and advanced cautiously, weapons never wavering. When the vac-suited strangers were within arm's length, one of them removed a helmet.

It was an Artaldean woman. She shook her head, letting her long, wavy black tresses tumble out of the coil beneath her helmet. With flawless caramel skin and a warm smile, Cheska felt strangely drawn to this woman, like some force of nature tugging on her.

"Jak," the woman said, nodding her head once.

"Del. Been a while," Jak said nonchalantly.

Del shook her head, as if in amazement, then burst forward and planted a deep kiss on Jak's mouth. Dr. Foehner looked shocked. Cheska was too.

They stayed locked at the lips for a long while, then broke their embrace. Del motioned to the people behind her and they took off their helmets. All

Artaldean. And there was one person Cheska recognized—Taro!

Jak held Del's hand, fingers intertwined, and turned back to Cheska and Dr. Foehner. "This is Delfina Cifuentes, my life-partner."

THE RESISTANCE

"WHY DIDN'T YOU GO WITH her?" Cheska asked.

Jak smiled sadly. "I wanted to. But when Del's abilities were discovered we didn't have much time to react. We faked her death and I got help from friends to smuggle her body to the surface. I had to stay behind to make sure there were no loose ends and nothing could track back to her. I couldn't even contact her. I knew the Aoratos were down here, but I couldn't risk it. We had to say goodbye."

"And now we get so say hello," Delfina said, squeezing his hand. Cheska saw how cloudy her eyes were, but she held it together—brave woman.

Delfina escorted them into an underground bunker, deep beneath what she called Mount Mandirama.

"It means sanctuary, in an old Earth language called

Nepali," Delfina said, as they walked down a seemingly endless stone incline, sliding ever deeper beneath the mountain.

"Old Earth?" Cheska asked.

Delfina turned back and smiled shaking her head. "Oh, you have a lot to catch up on, Cheska."

"So it seems," Cheska said, looking to Jak.

Jak gave her a shrug. "Don't look at me, kiddo. I haven't seen my girl in twelve years. I have a lot to catch up on too."

"Who built this facility?" Dr. Foehner asked.

"We did," Delfina said, "The Aoratos—the resistance. Aoratos means the invisible,"

"Resistance?" Dr. Foehner said, more to herself than anyone else.

Taro had been walking beside Cheska but had said very little. "So you're real," Cheska said, trying to break the ice.

"Um, yeah." Taro patted his flat black armor. "I think so?"

"I wasn't sure if all that had been a dream or not," she said.

"I thought the sour milk test proved I was real?"

Cheska grinned. "Yeah, sorry about that."

"A girl has to know if the man of her dreams is real, right?" Taro smirked.

She scowled at him. He was even more handsome and charming in person, and he had a mischievous glint in his eye. She liked that.

The incline finally leveled out into a great cone-shaped cavern, the neck of which, seemed to flow straight up the mountain and out the top. Cheska thought she saw a glimmer of daylight peeking back at her through the peak.

The walls of the cavern, at the base of the cone, were riddled with holes. As they walked through the cavern, Cheska noted that these holes, hundreds of them, were actually little hangers, each populated with some kind of craft. "What are those?" she asked Delfina.

"We have to have some way to travel around the planet. They're gravbikes. Fast, and they can reach orbit —assuming you have a breather and suit on." Delfina grinned.

When they had crossed the vast expanse of the cavern they arrived at a set of massive blast doors, at least five-meters square each. Without Delfina touching anything, the doors began to rumble open, each sliding sideways. Dust fell from cracks and ledges as the great maw opened. Cheska gaped at the thickness of the doors—each had to be a meter thick.

After the blast doors, they passed through an airlock before entering the facility proper.

"You can take your breathers off now," Delfina said. 'The atmosphere down is here is safe for humans."

"Humans?" Cheska asked.

"That's what you are, Cheska. Come, I'll explain everything. I promise."

The tunnel after the airlock was about ten-meters in diameter and moved off in a never ending curve to the right. A canal to their left was filled with water—a reservoir, perhaps. Judging by the arc of the canal,

Cheska guessed it might ring the base of the mountain. Dim green lights were set into the ceiling at regular intervals. They looked like biochem units.

Every so often Cheska noted shafts going vertically up and down, accessed by ladders set into the walls. There were also what amounted to bulkheads, every few hundred meters that separated the tunnel completely, and she suspected the water supply as well. Smart, that way a breach wouldn't contaminate everything.

After at least an hour's walk-or, hobble, for Cheska, they arrived at another airlock facing inward. They passed through it and into a great open cave, that seemed to have sunlight streaming down from the ceiling, but not that of a red dwarf, it was a yellow sun —like their home-world.

"Welcome to Sanctuary," Delfina said.

Cheska gasped. Hundreds of Artaldeans milled about—laughing, smiling, talking—living.

***

They stood in what Cheska knew was a cave. But cave was not the right word. Cave did not do this staggering space justice. It stretched out for what seemed kilometers. The ceiling hung decorated with gargantuan stalactites, interspersed with engineered arches.

Here and there massive columns reached up to the cave ceiling. Each of them speckled with lights.

"Apartments," Delfina said, leaning toward Cheska.

"You built these?" She asked.

"Most. The cave was here, but we've expanded and built over the decades."

Sanctuary was nothing like Ngome City. It lacked the

brilliance and glitter of the skyscrapers. It also lacked the dingy and repressed feeling of the city's underbelly. This was something more natural.

Streets lined with lower buildings ran off into the distance. They were crude structures to be sure, but they exuded a feeling of home. Places where you eat dinner with family, not the pristine meeting places of Ngome City's elite.

An older man, maybe in his thirties, made his way over to them. He had wavy dark brown hair, olive skin and fine features.

"Welcome," he said with an inviting smile.

Delfina cleared her throat. "This is Gai- um- our surgeon, Dr. Gaios Mavros,"

He nodded at Delfina who turned away. "And I suppose you must be my patient?" Dr. Mavros said, addressing Cheska.

Cheska nodded. "Yep, that would me."

The Doc had Cheska's knee mended on the spot in minutes with a sub-dermal manipulator. Apparently it had only been a torn meniscus, which was easily regenerated.

She extended her knee and put weight on it—like new. "Feels great, thanks, Doc."

"My pleasure. I have a few things to attend to, but I'll be at your briefing later." With that, Dr. Mavros walked off.

"Briefing?" Cheska asked Delfina.

"Like I said, we have a lot to fill you in on. Let's get you fed first. Unless you're not hungry?"

"Savior no!" Dr. Foehner said. "I'm famished."

Jak shrugged. "I suppose I could eat."

Cheska punched him hard on the shoulder, and as usual, she winced and rubbed her wrist.

"Hey now, kiddo. You don't want to have to get the Doc back again, do ya?" Jak grinned.

***

They ate well. The Aoratos put on a buffet with a spread of fresh foods, the like of which, Cheska had never seen. Sure, they had greenhouses on the *Ghimorphos*, but not with variety like this. She realized that she'd never been truly hungry before her sojourn to Sanctuary. Meals on the *Ghimorphos* were satisfying, balanced, and regular. Cheska vowed to never take food for granted again. She wondered what her mother might be eating. That thought was like a kick in the stomach. She shook it off. *"Not now,"* she thought. *"But I will find you, mum. I promise."*

After five days of running for their lives, dodging strange aliens—well, technically, she was the alien—and generally being miserable, it was a blessing to sit among so many happy smiling people. The buffet was held in a large open room. Guests and residents alike sat on long benches, cafeteria style, much like on the ship.

"So, I'm Abhuman?" Cheska asked Delfina out of the blue, continuing to chew on some type of bread.

Delfina smiled patiently. "Our slave masters—and that is what they are—call people like you Abhuman. It means away from human. Like I said before, we," she motioned to all the people around her, "are human. We are not Artaldeans. But I'll get back to that. You were born with a genetic mutation that gives you certain gifts.

You have the ability to manipulate space and time. You're a bender."

Cheska had to refrain from shouting that they were a curse.

"Usually," Delfina continued, "they manifest at puberty. Which of course can be quite a shock for the person. We've been brainwashed to think that such gifts are aberrations, and a form of demonic possession. Nothing could be further from the truth. You have no curse. In fact, Abhumans, or what we call Metahumans, are the key to freeing humanity."

Cheska's mind felt thick. "And what does all this have to do with Taro? Why could we contact each other in dreams, or whatever that was?"

Seated across from Cheska, Taro smiled when she asked about him. "Let me show you," he said. From one of the serving trays, he picked up a wilted pink blossom that had been garnish and had suffered from being close to the heat. Its leaves shriveled and its petals curled in on themselves. "Give me your hand," he said.

Cheska was suspicious, but stretched out her hand. Taro turned it over, palm up and placed the half-dead blossom in the center of her hand. Then he covered her hand with both of his hands, one above and one below. His hands were so warm. Her heart started to race. He held her gaze for a moment, looking deep into her eyes. Suddenly she felt a tingle throughout her body. Wow, she'd never felt that before.

Slowly he slid his bottom hand away, gently stroking the back of her hand as he did. She swallowed hard. Then he lifted his top hand. Her breathing went from shallow to full stop.

The flower was pinker, its leaves greener, its petals fuller. It could have just come off a live tree. "Great Savior," Cheska whispered.

The whole time Taro held her gaze. "Nope. That was all me." He smiled. "I'm a mender. I can stimulate growth in organic material."

"Taro is also Metahuman," Delfina said.

Cheska's smiled grew.

Dr. Foehner cleared her throat. "Delfina, we saw- creatures- on the surface. Not just creatures, but ruins, corpses. Do you know anything about them?"

Delfina's face went slack, taking on a look of profound sadness. She nodded weakly. "I do."

"I thought the planet was biologically sterile before we began terraforming? I saw detailed survey reports," Dr. Foehner said.

"You saw more theater, Doctor. One more piece of fiction. The creatures—we don't know what their species is called—had an advanced civilization here on Krijese. Not quite star-faring, but a harmonious, art loving, and peaceful culture thrived here."

"How did any of them survive?" Cheska asked.

"They're resilient," Delfina said. "Pockets of them hid when the terraforming started. Some built underground bunkers," she waved her hands around, "as we did here. Others found other ways to survive. Initially they had no weapons, save for makeshift items fashioned from tools. They aren't very good at fighting back, but they try. They are good at surviving though. Our terraforming activities have ruined their atmosphere, making it all but unbreathable for them. Any you encounter now would be wearing vacuum or environmental suits. The Aoratos tried to forge an alliance with them decades ago, but they don't trust us at all. Communication is difficult, and our encounters were not always peaceful."

"So, we just leave them to die?" Cheska asked.

"We tried, Cheska," Delfina said.

Cheska couldn't shake the image of the corpses of the parents and the small children. The Artaldean people, however unwitting, had devastated this planet. Wasn't it their responsibility to fix it?

***

After dinner Taro took Cheska on a tour of the Sanctuary. It was much larger than she had imagined. Delfina had been modest. They'd somehow managed to hollow out a big part of the mountain.

"I've been wondering, how did the Aoratos manage to keep this base whole, let alone a secret? I mean, we've been vectoring comets and meteorites into the planet. What if one struck the mountain?"

"We'd know in advance and be able to nudge it out of the way," Taro said.

"Sure, but even if it wasn't a direct hit, a near miss would surely ruin the land around the mountain?"

"Look around." He gestured to the corridors, and bulkheads and thick rock walls. "We're completely self-contained in here. The Sanctuary was built to the same standards as a starship, or orbital base. And we haven't always kept completely hidden. A few of the terraforming crew have stumbled onto us over the years."

"I never heard anything about it," Cheska said.

"No offense, but you didn't even know you were human until today."

Cheska scowled. "Thanks for the reminder."

"But to answer your question, we have other means to ensure that we don't have repeat visitors."

Cheska felt a lump form in her stomach. "You don't … kill them? Do you?"

"No, no. We just make sure they don't remember they were ever here."

"How is that even possible?" she asked.

Taro threw his hands wide. "How is giving life to a dying blossom possible? Or stopping time and freezing an entire shuttlecraft?"

She nodded. "Point taken." Score one for Taro.

***

They made their way to the briefing room after her tour of the facility. They were a bit late and the rest of the Aoratos and her companions were already seated.

"Sorry," Taro said. "Orienting the new person." He offered Delfina a wide grin but she waved him off.

"Let's get started," Delfina said. "You all know who I am. For the new arrivals, let me tell you what I do here. I'm the Sanctuary Prime."

The designation of Prime meant the head of something, like Dr. Foehner was the Gravitics Prime on the *Ghimorphos*.

"So basically, everything that happens in this facility is my fault," Delfina said with a smile. "You've already met our Medical Prime, Dr. Gaios Mavros." He nodded. "I'll introduce you to the other Primes, all of whom report directly to me. We have, at last count, 6,295 human residents."

That peaked Cheska's curiosity. "Why the distinction human residents?"

Delfina smiled. "Smart young woman. We also have seven Metahuman residents."

"More that Taro?" Cheska asked.

"Indeed. You'll meet them all. I'm assuming you'll stay?" Delfina asked.

That was a good question, Cheska mused. She hadn't wanted to stay on Krijese. But then where? She had no other home. She had no home-world. The *Ghimorphos* had been the only home she'd ever known—she'd been born there. "I- I don't know. What about my mother? She's still on the *Ghimorphos*."

"We're working to free all the Artaldeans, Cheska. In the meantime, you'll be safe here," Delfina said. "Now, let's begin your reeducation. "Where to start?" she mused. "With the Cataclysm, I suppose."

The mere mention of the word turned Cheska's stomach. Artaldeans avoided discussing it, as it triggered their genetically coded sensory response, recalling the full and visceral horror.

"I'm sorry, I know mentioning it is unpleasant, and we'll be able to fix that. But the whole Cataclysm is a lie. Oh, there was a cataclysm, but it was nothing manmade. Several centuries ago—we're not sure exactly—a race of spacefaring creatures called the Tarbizhad arrived at Earth. Unfortunately for our ancestors, we were a perfect food source for them."

"What?" Dr. Foehner said, with a horrified look on her face.

"Bear with me, people. It's an unpleasant story. Let me finish, then ask all the questions you like. We proved to be much more than a food source. We were apparently very palatable to them, but unlike previous food sources, we were sentient, advanced beings. Twice as good. They harvested millions of our people, then the Tarbizhad decimated the planet with terrible weapons. That is the cataclysm you remember. But we humans were not the cause. We were the victims."

Even Jak looked stunned at this point. Cheska didn't know how much of this story he knew already, but it appeared he hadn't known he was on the menu.

The Tarbizhad," Delfina continued, "are ruthless beyond reckoning. They enslave other highly intelligent races and make them clients. Serve the Tarbizhad, or become food. It's a simple choice in those terms, I suppose. One of the client races happened to have a mastery of genetic and engrammatic manipulation. The short version is that they erased our humanity—religions, language, everything. And then supplanted that identity with one they manufacture wholesale. The Artaldeans. The Covenant. The Apocalypse. All of it. Pure fiction. A genetically encoded narrative designed to enslave us."

Cheska thought she should be horrified, but she kept being told things that were inuring her to further shock. Just when she thought things couldn't get any worse, they took a quantum leap.

"As a demonstration of the contempt they feel

toward us, they called us Artaldean. It means flock. Or herd. As in a herd of animals to be eaten, culled, bread, and generally used. Maybe they have a perverse sense of humor?" Delfina shrugged. "I don't know."

"Do they look like us?" Jak asked.

"We don't know," Dr. Mavros said, "none of us has ever seen one."

"Here's another fun question," Delfina said. "Where are all the scientists?"

"The *what?*" Dr. Foehner asked.

That seemed random and just plain weird, Cheska thought.

"People who explore the fundamental questions of nature?" Dr. Mavros offered.

"We're taught in school that the Savior revealed all to us," Cheska said.

"Lies. Where do you think all of the technology comes from? Starships? Gravitics?" Delfina asked.

"Gifts from the Savior?" Cheska said tentatively.

Delfina smiled. "That's what they'd have you believe. They train *engineers*, like Dr. Foehner. But what you are able to learn has been genetically limited. There are questions you don't ask—can't ask. They've excised that ability. They used to do something called *gelding* to male cattle. It made them more docile, easier to control."

"Gelding?" Cheska asked.

Delfina smirked. "You probably don't want the details so close after dinner. Now, let's move forward in time, maybe a century. Our ancestors had been food, slaves, and entertainment for the Tarbizhad. We were programmed to be as docile as sheep, and were none the wiser. We were happy in our ignorance. Then came a secret ally. Another client race of the Tarbizhad. They too were enslaved, but given their highly technical role in genetics, they were the ones who designed the human re-programming—against their will of course. This meant that there was nobody to re-program this other race."

"What are they called?" Cheska asked.

"They prefer to remain anonymous for now, working behind the scenes, as it were. But our benefactors were quite unhappy with what the Tarbizhad were doing to them, humanity, and all the other races and species that these foul creatures preyed upon. They saw humanity as the perfect vessel for a new weapon against the Tarbizhad. They introduced minor mutations in our genome over a century. They are masters of obfuscation, and even the brightest Tarbizhad had no clue what was happening in the human genome over the decades. Finally, the first Abhuman was born. She manifested telepathic abilities at puberty. Sadly her life was cut short when the Tarbizhad discovered this *aberration*. What they deemed Abhuman. Thereafter, our benefactors built a support system for any new Abhuman. Such that when one emerged, they could be shepherded, and groomed."

"I'm sorry, but how is what these benefactors do, any better than what you claim the Tarbizhad are doing?" Dr. Foehner asked.

"Fair question, Doctor. Let me be blunt. The alternative is you remain a slave. We remain slaves—the entire human race." Delfina let that statement hang for a while and nobody spoke.

"What now, Del?" Jak said.

"We try to stay alive, my love."

***

How is a person supposed to react when they find out their entire existence is a fabrication? Some sick joke. A cruel prank played on an unwitting opponent? Cheska ran through these scenarios the next day as she lay on an inclined bed in the Sanctuary's infirmary.

Cheska was a bit concerned when Dr. Mavros came to her with the hypospray. "Is this going to hurt?"

"No. It shouldn't hurt. You might be a bit confused for awhile," Dr. Mavros said.

"Might? As in … you don't know for sure?" Cheska asked.

"We only have two doses of the serum," Delfina said. "One for Taro, and one for you."

"Why him? Why me?" Cheska asked, feeling a bit panicked, if she were being honest with herself.

"It's another very long story. Will you trust me?" Delfina asked.

Jak nodded at Cheska.

Could she trust her? She barely knew Delfina. Though she still felt that tug, that pull toward this woman she barely knew. She trusted Jak, and if he trusted her … "Ok."

Delfina nodded, and Dr. Mavros pressed the hypospray, injecting Cheska with a vial of blueish gel. She only felt a slight pressure on her skin.

Delfina placed a cold, dry hand on Cheska's arm and she flinched. "The serum contains an enhanced baseline human genome. It will remove much of the engrammatic conditioning imposed by the Tarbizhad, and will replace that with our species natural instincts. There's also an added component of genetic memory inserted by our benefactors. It contains a vast cultural database, including history, art, and language. It's certainly not a complete database—call it a vast snapshot of the culture. That knowledge will help you make sense of what we lost. Only you and Taro will possess that knowledge."

Cheska nodded nervously, waiting for convulsions, pain, or some drastic effect to take hold of her and kill her. But it didn't happen. What did happen, was that she could taste something—a fruit. "Apples," she said glancing at Delfina, then to Dr. Mavros.

"Good!" Dr. Mavros said.

Sensations:.

Sounds.

A scent of moss.

New words.

Countries.

Religions? My God!

Gods?

Suddenly, it was all there.

Fragments of memories from a millions of people, hundreds of countries, and thousands of societies. All jammed into her brain. She knew it all, or rather, felt it all—sort of. To appreciate something, all she had to do was actively think about it. She wanted to recall everything, all at once! It was amazing! She had answers to questions she hadn't known existed.

Suddenly she felt light headed and heard Dr. Mavros shouting something. His face started to fade.

"Breathe, Cheska! Breathe!" Dr. Mavros shouted.

She felt a mask on her face. "What happened?" Cheska asked.

"You started to pass out—forgot to breath," Dr. Mavros said.

"Wow!" Cheska said. She remembered how the Tarbizhad had erased all language from the memories of the initial human breeding stock, replacing them with a single constructed language, free from any seditious words and concepts.

She remembered languages like English, Spanish, and Hindi. There were thousands. She couldn't speak them all, but she could manage quite a few. What the Artaldeans spoke was a language the Tarbizhad had designated *common*.

Cheska Bellamy was no longer feeling like a sixteen-year-old girl; she felt like she carried the whole history and knowledge of the human race, thousands of years old.

What was she becoming?

Total Recall

AFTER TARO UNDERWENT THE PROCEDURE, he and Cheska sat together quietly in a small side garden, a space just big enough for two. They looked at each other with the eyes of an old married couple. They were the only two people in the galaxy that knew what it truly meant to be human.

The Aoratos who'd had the Covenant conditioning removed, were on their way to becoming more human, but only Cheska and Taro had the perspective of an entire culture instantly available to them.

Cheska felt an itching on the back of her hand as they continued to stare at each other, not talking, attempting to communicate everything through an intense period of eye-to-eye contact. Her hand itched again, and when she reached down to scratch it, she noticed a fresh green sprout had grown from the plant nearest her, all the way over her hand, and was tickling it.

She looked up and scowled at Taro, who tried to look innocent, then broke out laughing.

"Two can play that game, Mr. Abhuman." She grinned at Taro while two sprigs of tall grasses hung from behind his ears.

"What are you smiling at?" he asked.

When a spring of grass fell and Cheska giggled, he figured it out.

"Hey, no bending time! How can I tell what you're doing?"

"Oh, like your little ninja plant?"

"Ninja," he said. "I like the sound of that word. Ninja, ninja, ninja, ninja, ninja!" He bent over belly laughing.

Cheska affected a serious look and cleared her throat. "Ahem, I think we're supposed to save humanity?"

"Tomorrow."

She rolled her eyes. "Ok, tomorrow."

"Besides," Taro said, "I want to have some fun before my shift in the infirmary tonight. Big kids have to work you know!"

She laughed. It felt wasteful to spend time relaxing, but Cheska knew she needed it. She had to process all this new input, and spending time with the only person who understood what that meant, felt good. Besides, she was starting to like Taro. The man of her dreams, though?

***

As his scout-ship pierced the event horizon of the planetary jump-gate, a ruddy, dirty planet blossomed in his view-screen. Projected on corner of his HUD, an image of the jump-gate receded behind his ship. The shimmering surface of the event horizon, a window into another star system, evaporated. The jump-gate's two vertical posts floated in space like lonely sentinels.

It had been two years since Venator Osgar had been summoned to hunt down and kill an Abhuman. He was looking forward to the challenge. Not that he was a bloodthirsty man, but two years of idleness played on the mind, and the Venators had been engineered for that singular purpose—to hunt and exterminate aberrations in the Artaldean gene pool.

Venator Osgar was proud of his work, of how he'd helped maintain the purity of the species. It was a noble calling, and to be so blessed by the Savior was a great honor. He reveled in the vitality and accomplishments of his people. "And from you, all the families of the Verse shall increase." The Savior had told the first mother of the Artaldeans.

He nosed his ship up and out of the atmosphere, toward a shimmering light in the sky—the *Ghimorphos*, one of the Artaldeans terraforming and colonization ships.

In twenty-minutes he was docked at Hab-3, what the locals had named Ngome City, and walking toward Vox Castus's office. He didn't like the man—they'd met once before, and he knew the Vox was an amoral creature. By rights, Castus should be on Osgar's purification list.

He had to console himself with the fact that Castus must serve the Covenant well, otherwise he wouldn't be in his position. He had to trust the will of the Savior—to do otherwise would be sacrilege.

Venator Osgar stood before Castus's opaque glassteel door, waiting for the system to recognize him. Of course Castus made him wait, such were the little games that little men played.

"Come," came a voice through the door. The glassteel faded to translucent and slid sideways into the wall.

Osgar gave Castus a small bow. "Vox Castus. You summoned me?"

"I did, I did. Nice to see you, as always, Venator Osgar. Sadly, we always meet during a time of crisis." Castus affected a look of disappointment that did not fool Osgar. The Venators were designed to sense any deception by an Artaldean.

Osgar smiled weakly.

"On to business then," Castus said. "We have a situation."

"I gathered, Vox."

"Of course you did. We believe we have an emergent Abhuman. Nobody can say what happened exactly, but our Gravitics Prime, Dr. Foehner, was giving an orientation to the new adults when something strange happened—Dr. Foehner vanished before their eyes."

"Telepathic hypnosis, perhaps? Or a short duration mind wipe?" Osgar wondered aloud.

"Could be. We don't have any data."

"No data?" Osgar said surprised.

"None. No video, audio, scent, or even gravitic imprint."

That was truly shocking. "How is that possible?" Osgar asked.

"We would very much like to know. Two more people went missing. A new adult, named Cheska Bellamy. She was in the audience with her friend, a girl named Azara Misra. Ms. Misra told the Watchers that Ms. Bellamy had vanished at the same time Dr. Foehner had."

"And the third?"

"The Captain of the Watchers, Jakande Boro. He used to be a good man."

"Used to be?"

"We have sensor data of him, apparently, kidnapping both Dr. Foehner and this Cheska Bellamy person. We also have the dead body of another Watcher—shot with his own plasma gun."

Osgar was truly awed. Nothing like this had ever happened. Certainly, the occasional Abhuman emerged, there would be a struggle, and they would be dealt with, but never had an Artaldean been murdered in the process. This must be a particularly vile creature. Dr. Foehner? He'd have to study her file.

"Do we know where on the ship they are now, Vox? Or do we have a rough idea?"

"Oh, they aren't on the ship, my good Venator. Captain Boro stole a shuttle, with a full crew of four."

"Where would they go with a shuttle? They can't access a jump gate in such a small craft, and there are no planets in range." Except for the half formed

Krijese, he realized. His face formed a disbelieving frown. "They went to Krijese?"

Vox Castus nodded. "That's the only destination they could have reached. Conveniently, our sensors went into full diagnostic testing for thirty-minutes as they fled, so that's another problem we have to deal with—collaborators still on board. In any case, you should be able find them once you're down on the planet."

"How is that? It's a big planet? Surely we can scan for them from up here, narrow it down?"

"Sadly, no. As a consequence of our aggressive terraforming activities, there's a substantial amount of metallic and radioactive dust in the atmosphere. This interferes with any fine sensor readings. We can track an active shuttle, for example, but once a ship is below cloud cover ..." he shook his head, "we lose them. But with you on the ground, you should be able to penetrate the interference."

"Vox, respectfully, it's still an enormous planet. Without narrowing it down, it could take me a century to find them."

Castus grinned. "That won't be a problem."

***

Madchen Foehner absently ran her thumb over the tiny lump on the inside of her bicep, over her beacon. All Primes on the *Ghimorphos* had been implanted with them. In retrospect, she suspected it had more to do with keeping track of what she was up to, and less to do with ensuring her safety, as Vox Castus had said. She'd considered asking Dr. Mavros to remove it, but she wasn't sure how well news of her implant would be received. She should have told Jak about it while they were en-route to the Sanctuary, but she hadn't. She still couldn't, even though she entertained the thought.

But then, she didn't need to worry, did she? She was under a mountain of rock. No scanning technology she knew could penetrate such shielding.

***

Cheska and Taro changed over the next couple of days. As the full knowledge of humanity's past settled in, and they could truly internalize it all, it weighed heavy on them, distorted their worldview, like a black hole warping space-time.

The girl of sixteen, and the boy of seventeen, were now old souls. The weight of what they knew—what they understood— was sobering. They tried to hide it from the others, though Cheska thought it must be obvious. She'd never been bubbly, but now she felt downright dour.

She and Taro spent most of their free time together. Who else could they talk to? They grew very close, very quickly, which had surprised Cheska; she was glad to have him. Even Jak seemed a bit alien to her now. Without Taro … she shook off the thought. She still thought about her mother. Guilty pangs reminded her that she should be mourning their separation; but how could she? And it wasn't that she didn't feel it, it was just that she felt like she was betraying humanity by dwelling on her emotional state. She had a duty now. Or did she?

Today was weapons and armor training for Cheska, Jak, Dr. Foehner, and some new recruits. All now stood lined up at attention. They were in a gymnasium constructed on a massive scale—like everything in Sanctuary.

The gymnasium was a T-shaped facility divided up into several cavernous rooms. On the left, lay an open-plan room with padded floors for hand-to-hand combat. Straight ahead, stretched a room hundreds of meters long and dozens wide. It had obstacles to hide behind and a variety of targets designed for rifle and range work. A third room, on the right branch of the T, had been set aside for close-quarters and small-arms training. It was arranged like the compartments on a ship, with bulkheads, hatches, passageways, models of offices and living quarters. It also boasted robotic targets that popped up at random.

Presently, they were doing hand-to-hand training. In addition to the padded floors, this area had human-shaped targets and a variety of primitive weapons hanging on the walls.

Their instructor was a man named Rupinder Waghorn— "Call me Wag," he'd said. Courtesy of her implanted memories, Cheska now knew he was a descendant of a tribe of people called Sikhs—great warriors from the ancient land of India. Though she suspected he didn't know anything about his history. She'd have to explain turbans to him, and the five K's, or articles of faith.

Earlier in the day they'd been instructed on the use of the standard sidearm—the plasma pistol, which they'd been issued, and now wore in hip holsters. Currently, Cheska was brandishing a long double edged knife—another item they'd been issued as standard carry.

"Right, so there may be times when you have to get in close," Rupinder said.

Cheska raised a hand.

"Yes, Ms. Bellamy?" Rupinder said patiently.

"Why would we ever need a knife? If we have access to pistols? They're a close range weapon, right?"

Rupinder nodded slowly. "You may know more than I do about humanity, Ms. Bellamy, but I assure you, I know, much more about Abhumans. There will be times when your plasma rifle or pistol may not function." He turned to very dark skinned woman, who Cheska recognized as being of African ancestry. "Zula, a little help please?"

She nodded and approached. Rupinder drew his sidearm and fired into a target off in the distance. "Works right?" He asked the students. Nods all around seemed to assure him. "Ms. Bellamy?" He proffered the pistol to her.

She took it.

"Put a shot into that target," Rupinder commanded.

She did, though not as close to center as Rupinder had.

"Good. Now shoot Zula."

She turned to him with a smile, thinking he was mocking her. "Excuse me?"

"Shoot Zula. You speak common, right?"

"You really want me to shoot her?"

"Give it a shot. Pun intended," he said, deadpan.

Zula was a very serious looking woman. She was beautiful, but in a hard way. Her body, a tangle of corded muscle and deadly curves. Cheska would certainly not want to have to fight her. Cheska held the pistol at arms length and Zula squared her shoulders in front of the barrel.

Zula nodded to Cheska.

Cheska began to feel the trigger a little bit with her index finger, but couldn't quite manage to pull it.

"Shoot her!" Rupinder ordered.

Cheska flinched, startled by the harsh command.

"Shoot her, now!" he shouted, his face almost touching hers.

So she did. Or tried to. She pulled the trigger, once, then twice, and even a third time. Nothing. There was only a sizzling popping noise. She glanced over to Rupinder then back to Zula, who was smirking.

"My good friend Zula here, is deadly with a blade. She can carve you up like a roast. But more importantly, she is also cyber. Her particular gift is called cyberkinesis."

Cheska understood the word on an intellectual level, given her newly expanded vocabulary. The root of the word, cyber, was from the ancient language called Greek, and meant skilled in steering or governing. It more commonly meant machine, or electronic system. The suffix of the word was also Greek, denoting movement or motion.

Rupinder must have sensed that Cheska was puzzling over the word. "It means," he said, "that Zula can control machines—anything with electronics."

Cheska was impressed.

"Now, Ms. Bellamy. While you are in my classes I

expect that the next time I give you a direct order," he leaned in nose-to-nose with Cheska, so close she grimaced at the odor of his breath, "that you bloody well follow it!" he finished with shout.

"Yes, sir, Wag."

He nodded curtly then moved down the line of students. "Now, as I was saying, when you need to get in close …"

***

The tiny scout ship speared Krijese's atmosphere like a javelin. Its black organic form like the shadow of a squid on the hunt.

When Venator Osgar pierced the lowest cloud layer, a tone alerted him to the homing beacon's direction.

A short flight took him into view of a soaring mountain. Very strange. The mountain was quite out of place with the surrounding ranges. Though, Dr. Foehner's beacon was registering as deep beneath it. Despite the hundreds of meters of dense rock, an aphasic-chrono-beacon transmitted a signal across a band of space and time, millions of years wide, such that on some frequencies—in some times—there was no mountain between the beacon and the scout ship. Time traveling radio signals—his masters were clever.

Killing the Abhuman would be easy now that he'd found her. Now, how the Core was he going to get inside?

***

Cheska and Taro had been spending a lot of time in the arboretum among a stunning array of trees from Earth, according to Delfina. The arboretum ringed Sanctuary.

It was nice to look at, but also helped scrub the air of carbon-dioxide.

Amid the sweet scent of blossoms and the musky scent of mosses and leaves, they walked and talked.

The air circulators generated a light artificial breeze, causing the leaves to whisper. Today, they would experiment with Cheska's abilities.

Cheska had been practicing her newfound bender powers as often as she had free time, which had been rare enough. There was a surprising amount of training required to be in the Aoratos resistance. Pistols, knives, rifles, hand to hand, armor … and she had thought working under Dr. Foehner was going to be a challenge.

She'd decided to play down her abilities to Delfina and the other Aoratos. She wasn't sure why, but she didn't feel like she could quite trust them. Taro and Jak were the only ones. She'd told Taro it was woman's intuition, which he'd thought quite funny, until she stopped time and dumped a vase of water on his head. Now *that* had been funny.

It turned out that not only could she stop time, or more accurately, move herself out of time, but she could also travel backward in time—though only for about a second. But that was still an ability with a lot of potential. Delfina said she was supposed to be able to manipulate space as well, though it hadn't worked yet. Maybe she didn't get that part of the ability? Had she forgotten to fill out some à la carte menu when she was little?

Cheska could see space-time, see quantum gravity, just like she could feel heat, or smell a flower. It was a sense she was unused to tapping into deliberately, and it was taking some getting use to, but the possibilities were really exciting.

"Bender experiment one," Taro said. He loved to dramatize things, and Cheska enjoyed his enthusiasm.

He produced a white pebble from his pocket. "I'm going to hide this white rock in one of my hands. You choose the correct hand, and I might let you kiss me."

Cheska snorted. "You might let *me* kiss you?"

He shrugged. "I might," he said with a straight face, placing his hands behind his back for a moment, presumably to switch the stone around, then extended his fists.

"Left," she said.

He rolled his eyes. "Lucky guess." He opened his hand to reveal the white stone. "You won. You may kiss me."

"No, no thanks." Cheska suppressed a snicker.

"Saving them up for later, huh? Smart." He repeated the procedure.

"Left, again."

He frowned. "Are you cheating?"

She laughed. "Of course I am, that's the point!"

"Try again."

Cheska focused again, and took a breath. She allowed herself to see the multi-colored mandala, that was the stream of space-time permutations. So many colors, shapes. Her brow wrinkled as she homed in on one tiny spec—one of an almost infinite number of futures. It kept slipping from her grasp. Pressure spiked in her brain as she mentally thrust forward. There. She saw what she was looking for, releasing her grip on local-space-time, her awareness returned to her previous time.

"Right," she said.

"Damn! Again."

"Left."

Taro exhaled. "We need to make this harder." He wiggled his jaw side to side. "Hmm. Ok, I'll hide the stone somewhere in this room. You leave, close the door, then I'll shout when you can come back in. Got it?"

"Got it."

"No peeking!"

Cheska shook her head solemnly. "Never." She left. Taro shouted. She returned.

She wiped sweat from her brow, feeling light-headed. "Under the blue planter, by the door."

"No way! Again."

The tests were tiring for Cheska. Each loop sapped a lot of her endurance. It was like running laps on a track.

By test number twenty-two, she'd decided to call it a day, feeling fatigue unlike any she had ever experienced. Her nose had also begun to bleed. That couldn't be good.

"So, you can see the future," Taro said, shaking his head in amazement. "Cool."

"No, I cannot see the future. I can test permutations of the timeline in very short intervals. That's not even close to the same thing."

"Yeah, you can see the future."

Cheska threw up her hands. "I give up."

Taro cocked his eyebrows and pointed at her. "You realize I owe you twenty-two kisses?"

***

Delfina woke to a churning stomach. She bolted out of bed. Jak stirred beside her.

She yanked open the door to the bathroom and emptied her stomach into the toilet. She gagged and coughed as she tried to get it all out.

A hand pulled her hair back. "You ok, babe?" Jak asked.

She shook her head as she gagged again. This was the second morning she'd been sick. What had she eaten? Oh gods. It hadn't been the food. She'd missed her period last month but hadn't thought anything of it … until now. Jak hadn't been back long enough for *that* to happen.

She dropped to her knees, hands shaking as she gripped the edge of the toilet bowl.

"*Not this. Not now,*" she whispered.

Umbral

<hr>

VENATOR OSGAR HAD BEEN SURPRISED to find the tunnel. There were not supposed to be any structures built on Krijese, yet, here it was. And Dr. Foehner's ac-beacon was somewhere beneath the mountain. Why had Vox Castus not told him about this place? Surely he knew? He mulled over the possibilities as he stood, back flat against the stone wall, just to the right of the titanic blast doors. The active-camouflage of his hunter-suit engaged, he would be virtually invisible to any passersby.

He'd waited for three days, standing absolutely still. Such a feat was beyond an Artaldean, but not for the highly engineered Venators.

He felt a vibration in his feet then heard the great doors rumble to life, grinding sideways. Bits of dust fell from the top of the doors and settled on his hunter-suit, it tried to compensate, but the suit too was vibrating from the motion of the doors.

Six armed and armored Artaldeans filed out of the gigantic doors and marched up the long tunnel to the surface. Who were these people? They were not Covenant. The markings on their suit were unfamiliar to him. He'd have to file that image for Vox Castus.

Osgar waited until the doors began closing and slipped in. He had a job to do.

***

Supper was a family affair at the Sanctuary, and truly, that's how these former strangers were starting to feel to her. Call it shared suffering, or whatever, but they had a bond. She smiled as her eyes took in all the twenty smiling faces per side of her table.

Cheska had to admit to herself; despite the weight of all the knowledge she now carried in her head, coming to Sanctuary had been a blessing. No, not a blessing, she had to purge that kind of thinking—attributing all good to some Savior, which turned out to be an illusion created by a psychotic race of aliens. There had been saviors in humanity's past, and there had been benevolent gods—or at least the stories of them. The Christians had one, the Jews, the Muslims, and the Hindus had many—the list was as long as human history. But did they really exist? Would she ever meet one? Maybe they could help overthrow the Tarbizhad …

"What are you thinking about?" Taro asked, startling her.

"Nothing important."

"You know, that I know, when you're lying. Right?"

She rolled her eyes. Score two for Taro. The comps —she and Taro—also had a telepathic bond. Not full on telepathy like Felicia had, but they could sense each other's emotions—even from vast distances. He placed a hand on top of hers. She closed her eyes to soak up that simple, powerful touch. He gave her hand a squeeze then picked up his fork again, taking another bite of salad.

Dr. Foehner was asking Delfina how she'd been discovered as an Abhuman, so Cheska tuned in to that conversation.

Delfina took a deep breath. "Well, an Abhuman's powers emerge along the lines of their natural gifts. For example, Cheska, you have a knack for physics. Your abilities seem to revolve around the control of time. That's not by accident. Our benefactors amped up the genes we already had, rather than introduce something totally foreign which the Tarbizhad might have detected. Back to Dr. Foehner's question- "

"Call me Madchen, please," Dr. Foehner said. "I think after all we've been through we're on a first name basis?"

Cheska now knew that Madchen meant maiden in the old Germanic languages. She enjoyed these little flashes of insight. Language was so fundamental to a culture—to erase language was to truly erase the people, as the Tarbizhad had intended.

Delfina smiled. "Madchen it is. I worked as a genetic and engrammatic engineer. Very rarely, we had cases where a fetus presented with some defect—perhaps caused by the mother's exposure to radiation on assignment, or even random mutation. My job was to fix those. And given the rarity of that role, I also specialized in engrammatic resequencing."

Brainwashing, Cheska registered. Damn.

"They call me an engro. My Abhuman abilities emerged along the lines of memory manipulation," Delfina continued. "It took years for me to recognize that anything was wrong. I simply thought it was convenient that my parents seemed to forget things I wanted forgotten, or knew things I wanted them to know." She shrugged, smiling. "Every girl's dream, right? So, naturally, I tested high in bio-engineering. I discovered the true nature of my abilities when I was assisting with the autopsy of an apparent accidental death. I began to get visions of the dead man's last moments. He'd been murdered. Executed, actually, by one of the Venators. At the time I understood that the Venators were tasked with hunting down Abhumans— what we call Metahumans. But this man had no abilities that I could see from his memory. Apparently the dead man had crossed one of the Voces. Vox Castus was his name."

Cheska shuddered. She knew she had despised that weasel for a good reason, she just hadn't known what it was.

"So he had the man assassinated," Delfina continued. "I found I could pull memories from the dead, as well as pull or alter the memories of the living. I managed to keep it secret for quite a while. I investigated what the Tarbizhad were doing, but eventually I knew too much. I was dying inside a little each day, knowing what they were, what we had become. I had to try to stop them." She shook her head, her eyes teary. "Anyway, that's when I was discovered. Jak and I had been paired for a few years, but hadn't had any children, so he helped fake my death, in fact, he made it look like he'd killed me. Which earned him a promotion apparently." She smiled at Jak. "Congratulations, love." She turned back to the rest of the table. "My poor Jak had to stay behind to cover up our deception. He agreed to help identify and aid new Abhumans that emerged."

It hit Cheska like a bolt of lightning and she spun on Jak. "You knew what I was?"

He nodded slowly.

Then it dawned on her—his sudden appearance and friendship; she'd been an assignment. "Why the hell didn't you tell me?" The foreign curse word seemed to confuse him.

He shook his head slowly and made to speak a few times, but said nothing.

Delfina rescued him. "He was ordered not to."

"By who?" Cheska demanded.

"By the Aoratos Prime."

"And who is that?"

"None of us have met him ... or her," Delfina said.

Cheska had no facial expression to convey the utter frustration she felt. "What? You're kidding me right? You have another *savior* that you've never met? Are you people stupid? Or just suckers for punishment?" Cheska stood up from the table abruptly, sending her plate clattering to the floor. She also caught the top of her new sidearm on the edge of the table, yanking it back in frustration.

Taro put out a hand, but Cheska shrugged it off. "Don't!"

***

Cheska was in a truly foul mood when Taro came into her room and plopped down on the end of her bed. She was sitting on her pillow cross-legged, scowling at nothing in particular.

"Everything is a lie," she said flatly.

Taro's face looked pained, like he was struggling to find the right words, but said nothing.

"Have you ever lied to me, Taro?"

He looked wounded. "I don't think so. Not deliberately, anyway."

"Can we keep it that way? Please?"

He nodded.

Taro was a good friend, maybe more than a friend. A good friend knew when to shut-up and just listen. Azara had known how to be a good friend. Cheska missed her desperately. What had Azara heard about her? She'd think Cheska was a Abhuman, possessed. And her mother? "Oh God," she moaned, dropping her face into her hands.

"I'm sure Jak did what he thought was best for you. He cares about you. You know that?"

Cheska lifted her head up slowly, like it weighed a ton. "It's not just him. It's everything. Me, the Covenant, the Aoratos. The Verse! Everything is messed up. What pisses me off, is that last week I thought I had all the rules to life figured out. Right?"

Taro nodded.

"I mean, sure, I wasn't crazy about every choice ahead of me, and less so about some of the lack of choices. But now … everything is spiraling down the gravity well."

Taro shuffled forward and put a hand on her knee.

Cheska leaned in and kissed him. She hadn't planned to, she just did it. She held it for a long moment then leaned back.

Taro looked dumbstruck.

"I- I'm sorry. I shouldn't have done that," she said.

"No," Taro said.

Her face felt flush, the weight of shame dragging her mood down lower.

Taro shook his head. "No, I mean, not no that you shouldn't have, no, as in, it was fine. More than fine." He smiled. He leaned in and he kissed her this time.

Brrramp! Brrramp! Brrramp! Brrramp! Brrramp! Brrramp! A Klaxon shattered the silence.

"What's that?" Cheska asked.

Taro looked disbelieving. "It's the intruder alarm." He stood up. "It could be a drill, they do them every once in a while. Let me check. You stay here." He jogged out her door.

"Like hell!" Cheska bolted after him.

Handfuls of the Aoratos were running down the corridors. "What's going on?" Taro shouted.

"Intruder!" One of them yelled back.

Taro scowled at her. "Cheska, seriously, you need to

stay here, where it's safe."

"Not happening. You forget, I'm part of the Aoratos now. I'm one of you. If there is an intruder, then it's my home that's being invaded too."

Several guards, wearing the now ubiquitous black body armor and carrying heavy rifles, formed up at the main doors to the outer ring of the Sanctuary. Cheska spotted Delfina and Jak running down a hall toward the guards.

Taro ran ahead to speak with Rupinder, their weapons instructor, and one of Taro's friends in the guard.

Dr. Foehner walked over to Cheska. "What's going on?"

"It's the intruder alert. And I don't think it's a drill."

Taro had a very worried look on his face as he spoke to Rupinder. He clapped his friend on the shoulder and walked back to Cheska and Dr. Foehner. "We have our first intruder."

"Just one?" Dr. Foehner asked.

Taro nodded. "We think so. And this person is hard to track. Probably wearing scout armor. He, or she, is still in the outer ring."

Cheska noted Jak and Delfina in rapid discussion with the guards. She turned back to Taro. "How many ways into the central part of Sanctuary?"

"Officially, one," Taro said.

"Unofficially?" Cheska asked.

"Lots. They designed Sanctuary to be secure, but also wanted us to be able to escape if something like this happened. If there was truly only one way in and out, it would be an easy thing to bottle us up in here."

Cheska caught a shadow out of the corner of her eye and snapped her head around. Nothing.

Jak jogged over to them. "Dr. Foehner, we're going to take you somewhere safe."

Dr. Foehner nodded. "What about Cheska?" putting a hand on her shoulder.

"She can take you. Cheska, can you look out for Dr. Foehner?" Jak asked.

"Jak," she protested, "I know I'm not a real Watcher or guard, but I want to help. Why bother giving me weapons training?"

"She's important to the Aoratos, kiddo. With her knowledge of gravitics, we could do a lot more for our people. The gymnasium is the safest spot. Take her there. Please?"

Jak had one of those faces that mixed kindness, reason, understanding, and then threw in a bit of guilt trip for good measure. How could she say no to anything he asked? She wanted to help, not be selfish. If Dr. Foehner was that important, then that's what she should do. She nodded.

Jak put a hand on Cheska's shoulder and gave it a gentle squeeze. "Be careful, ok?"

She'd felt distant from Jak since the memory implant, but just then she felt compelled to hug him, so she did.

"Hey now, I'm gonna be fine," he assured her.

"I know."

Taro leaned in and planted a kiss on her cheek. "See you soon."

She felt a flush. "C'mon, Doc. Let's get somewhere

safe."

***

Cheska and Dr. Foehner jogged toward the main gymnasium. Cheska did not like the idea of running from a fight. It then struck her how odd that feeling was. A couple of days ago, fighting had been abhorrent to her. She wouldn't have even thought to slap someone. Now she felt a burning desire for revenge. She wanted to find this intruder and punish them for everything the Tarbizhad had done to her people.

The feeling was as natural as basking in a sunbeam —then she realized she'd never actually basked in a sunbeam—she only felt such things because of the newly implanted memories. Strange, she truly was a new person.

"In here," she said to Dr. Foehner. This is where they'd done their weapons training.

Cheska secured the door and locked it, punching in a code provided by Jak. A loud clack sounded as several bolts slid into the locked position. The lighting in the facility was dimmed, providing just enough to find their way from room to room.

"Seems secure." Dr. Foehner offered with a shrug, and began wandering around the gymnasium. She slipped into the close-quarters small-arms training area. Cheska followed.

Dr. Foehner took a seat behind a desk. Suddenly, a robotic target popped up with a rifle aimed at her. She was startled for a moment and Cheska grinned.

"Bang. You're dead," Cheska said evenly.

Dr. Foehner laughed nervously.

Cheska slumped into the apparent guest chair.

"How are you faring, Cheska?"

"I guess I'm ok. All things considered."

"You and Taro seem to be getting on nicely?"

That embarrassed her. Taro was the first boy she had really felt something for, which she had only just realized at that moment. Determined to act the sum of her memories, and not her biological age, she nodded. "Yes, I suppose we are."

"He seems like a pretty good guy."

"I don't have a lot to compare him to, but I think so. And to think, next year I might have had a life-partner assigned to me." It occurred to Cheska to ask about Dr. Foehner. She'd been so wrapped up in what she'd lost, that she'd never asked about her partner, or children. Did she even have them? "Do you miss your partner? Your children?"

Dr. Foehner smiled weakly and shook her head. "I don't have either."

Now Cheska felt bad, her attempt at being considerate might have opened old wounds. "I'm sorry. Did something happen to him?"

"No, I never paired."

Now Cheska was confused, but even more curious. "Never?"

Dr. Foehner shook her head. "Privileges of rank."

Not that Cheska had really been enthused about being paired, but the thought of being alone, seemed … lonely? "Never found the right person?"

Dr. Foehner gave her a sad smile. "I did, but we'd never have been paired. And I didn't want to be with anyone else. So, I challenged the system, and given I had the highest test scores ever recorded for engineering, they gave in to me. I told them I wanted to wait, to spend more time looking for the right partner. The Confab indulged me. I dragged my heels for years, never intending to pick a partner. Eventually, I became critical enough to the project and busy enough, that the issue was forgotten."

"I'm sorry. But if they were going to let you choose someone, why not this person you loved? What happened to him?"

"*She* paired with someone else. She has children, and by all accounts is quite happy."

"Oh." Was all Cheska could manage when she realized the implication of Dr. Foehner's admission. "So you're …"

"Abhuman?" Dr. Foehner asked, finishing Cheska's question. "In a sense. Like you I was born different." She smiled.

"That must have been hard. Must still be."

She shrugged with gentle resignation. "No harder for me than many others. But at least my *deviation* could be easily hidden. I had no emergent powers popping up. So in that sense I had it easy."

Cheska suddenly felt a tingling in her entire body—she sensed something—someone. It was the same feeling that she had when she was near Delfina or Taro. They were both Metahuman.

"What is it?" Dr. Foehner asked.

"Someone's in here with us," Cheska whispered, drawing her plasma pistol. "Stay here!" Cheska crept out of the model office and made her way to the junction of the T-shaped facility. She poked her head around the right hand corner and into the rifle range section. The challenge with this area, was that it was deliberately filled with obstacles—an intruder could be hiding behind any of them.

If only she could sense where the tingling was coming from. But it was just a general sense, and not directional like hearing. Maybe if she concentrated? She ducked her head back out of the range. Taking a few breaths, she closed her eyes and let her mind relax, sinking into the surrounding sensations.

It was eerily quiet under the mountain. The density of the rock walls meant that sound was highly compartmentalized. Cheska reached out with her mind, trying to feel her way to the source of the tingling, where it might be stronger, more pronounced. Nothing.

Then she caught a distinctly industrial odor—light and oily—a weapon lubricant.

Cheska followed her nose.

***

Somehow these creatures had detected Venator Osgar, and barred their main door. They thought they had the hunter trapped. They were mistaken. They'd taken great pains to disguise a whole network of auxiliary entrances and exits, but they were easy for a Venator's senses to pick out. A Venator saw beyond the visual spectrum, well into the infrared and ultraviolet.

He watched the dance of heated currents of the air, seeping through the maze. They were barely wide enough for him to squeeze through, but nevertheless

103

seemed to permeate the entire base.

He crawled and squirmed through several branching tunnels, always following Dr. Foehner's ac-beacon. He was getting close. The beacon was below him now. He dropped down into some kind of training facility.

***

As she'd been taught, Cheska held the butt of her pistol close to her chest. Only when she was ready to fire would she extend her arm, align her sights, and shoot—the drill was ingrained in her mind—muscle memory now.

Cheska crept up on one of the synthetic obstacles. It was shaped like a rock formation, but made of some lighter, but more durable material—designed to take direct plasma fire without fracturing.

A shadow moved from behind the obstacle and Cheska fired. The shrill bark of plasma lit up the dim room and scorched the obstacle. She hadn't hit anything, but she most certainly had *seen* someone, something.

"I know you're there," she said. "Come out and I won't have to shoot you." She knew how ridiculous that sounded as soon as it passed her lips. She glanced from obstacle to obstacle—nothing.

The tingling coursed in her body now, much stronger than before. Cheska spun, but not in time. A shadowy hand chopped down onto her wrists, sending her pistol clattering to the floor.

A humanoid shape of utter blackness, of pure shadow, stood before her. Then a young woman coalesced out of the darkness, a pistol leveled at Cheska.

Cheska knew at that moment she was about to die.

105

SHADOWS IN THE DARK

THE OLIVE SKINNED WOMAN, MAYBE in her twenties, sported shoulder-length black hair, completely shaved on one side of her head. She was clad in a skin-tight suit of matte ebony.

The woman bowed. "Saturnina Villanueva, at your service, Ms. Bellamy. My friends call me Sat." She holstered her pistol.

What? Cheska was still waiting to be shot.

"Sorry for spooking you, but I was worried when you two went off alone. Figured I'd shadow you," she grinned, "if you'll excuse the pun."

Cheska gasped, finally realizing that she'd been holding her breath. "Wow. You ... Wow! You scared me. You're an ab-" she corrected herself, "Metahuman?"

"I am indeed. I'm a shade—umbralkinetic—I control shadow. Well, light really—I suppress it, bend it, shape it. That sort of thing."

A scream filled the newfound tranquility.

"Dr. Foehner!" Cheska bolted toward the office.

Cheska was panting by the time she entered the room. A shadowy man that looked a lot like Saturnina, loomed over Dr. Foehner, gripping her by one arm. She looked terrified.

"You're not the one," the shadowy man muttered at Dr. Foehner, then must have sensed Cheska and Saturnina and spun on them.

Saturnina began to shift from human form into shadow, but as she was transitioning, the man lunged at her, grabbing her neck. For a split second, the veins in the man's outstretched arm glowed a hateful red, like fiery ribbons of lava flowing outward to his hand. They snaked across his fingers into Saturnina's neck, a frantic rigor consuming her face.

He released her. She fell to the floor in a heap, scratching at her throat. He turned his attention to Cheska. "Two Abhumans?" He seemed surprised, but recovered quickly and thrust a hand at Cheska, but she was at least a full stride away.

She didn't even think about it, he just appeared to freeze. Shockingly, the red veins in his arm now extended a hand's length beyond his finger tips—wicked, ravenous tendrils.

Cheska grabbed Saturnina under the shoulders and dragged her out of the room. As she returned to get Dr. Foehner, she noticed the man's eyes moving slightly, as if he were resisting her ability. The red veins were continuing to spread across his hands and face, despite her stopping time. She didn't know if she'd be able to get Dr. Foehner to safety before he recovered.

By the time Cheska thought of shooting him, time had resumed its normal flow. She wasn't quite where he had expected, and he was disoriented for a moment. He recovered quickly, drawing a tiny pistol and firing. Cheska spotted the barrel flare of neon fuchsia light. It looked like a thin rod creeping out of his pistol. She realized she'd done it again—stopped, or slowed time. But the pistol had already been fired, its beam in action.

She easily sidestepped the shot and fired her own pistol, its orange plasma bolt also creeping, inexorably, out of her barrel. Her target, however, could not move. The flow of time resumed and her plasma bolt slammed into the man, knocking him off his feet, causing his suit to effervesce. The plasma bubbled across his suit. Shielding, she realized! Dammit!

"Dr. Foehner! Come on!" Cheska yelled.

The Doctor sprinted out of the room, but Cheska couldn't leave Saturnina. She stooped over Saturnina, but she wasn't breathing, her face lifeless mask of shadow, bloody veins painting her death-mask in vivid color.

"Cheska!" It was Jak's voice.

"Watch out, he- " she started.

The killer staggered out of the room, firing as he did.

Cheska tried to stop time, but she was too late. Jak was doubled over, grabbing his stomach.

She screamed, "No!" She didn't stop time, but she

moved inhumanly fast, faster than the assassin. She got around beside him and smiled as his face contorted in pain. She pulled the dagger out of his back—she'd buried it deep into his liver—the most painful target, and one where the victim was overwhelmed and couldn't cry out in pain. She'd been aghast when Rupinder had taught it to them, but now she was so glad he had.

"Bastard!" she cursed, and wept.

***

Cheska dropped the bloody dagger and went to Jak, slumping to her knees. He was still alive.

He tried to smile at her but grimaced instead, wincing. "Damn that hurts."

Cheska was sobbing now, but tried to laugh. "I thought big tuff guys like you didn't feel pain?"

"We feel it," he winced, "we just ignore it—most of the time." He winked.

Delfina and Dr. Mavros jogged into the room. Delfina dropped down at Jak's head and held his face. "*Jakande*," she whispered. She stroked his forehead.

"Ok, give me some room!" Dr. Mavros shouted.

Cheska and Delfina moved back. Delfina spun on the assassin, who lay dying in a pool of blood. "Did Jak get him?"

"No. I did," Cheska said, with no hint of emotion, all sorrow drained, spent.

"Good." Delfina made to kick the killer, then seemed to think better of it. She knelt beside the dying man and placed her hands on his temples. She stared into his cold eyes. "*Why?*" she whispered.

109

"Orders," he croaked.

"Who's?"

"The Confab, Vox Castus."

"That rat bastard! I will end him," Delfina said, through clenched teeth. "Why only send one of you?"

"Only after- the Doctor." His eyes flicked to Dr. Foehner who huddled in the corner of the room. "Didn't know about the others."

"The Doctor? Why the Doctor?" Delfina asked.

"Followed- beacon ... Wrong target," the assassin managed

Delfina turned on Dr. Foehner like a viper ready to strike. "A beacon?"

Dr. Foehner dropped her chin. "I- "

"Save it, I'll deal with you later!"

"I only wanted ... better world," the killer mumbled.

"A better world?" Delfina asked, her words dripping like molten metal. "Let me show you who your masters truly are!" She stared at him for a long while, holding his temples.

The killer began to sob, tears trickling out of the corners of his eyes. "No ... Savior forgive me."

"What did you show him?" Cheska asked.

"I showed him who he'd been really fighting for," Delfina said cruelly.

***

Cheska stood over Jak in the infirmary, Taro beside her, holding her hand.

"He looks awful," she said.

"He's a strong man, Cheska. And he loves you. He won't leave you. You wait and see," Taro said.

She appreciated his encouragement, but Jak's wounds were clearly mortal. Her new human memories told her that much. She knew Taro could puzzle that out as well. Though Taro had tried to heal Jak, the assassin's weapon had been imbued with the same virus that had killed Saturnina. It wasn't killing Jak outright, but it was preventing Taro from healing him.

"Why are we keeping that thing alive?" Cheska asked Dr. Mavros, pointing to the killer.

"Because, Delfina thinks she may be able to get more information out of him," Dr. Mavros replied.

"I thought she could do that even when they were dead," Cheska said bitterly.

Dr. Mavros didn't answer.

"C'mon Cheska, lets get out of here. Nothing you can do for him now," Taro said. He pulled up her hand that he was holding and kissed it.

Cheska stared at the covered body of Saturnina Villanueva. She thought she saw a shadow slip sideways and shuddered, turning her attention back to Sat—a girl she'd only just met.

Strangely, she felt so connected to her in death.

***

Dr. Gaios Mavros waited until Cheska and Taro were gone a few minutes, then made sure nobody else was close by. He glanced out the door of the infirmary and down both halls. Confident he was alone, he locked the doors and walked over to the assassin.

The man on the table was barely conscious. "I'm sorry, Osgar," Dr. Mavros said as he laid a hand on the assassin's neck. Bright red veins formed on Dr. Mavros's arm, creeping down his hand and onto Venator Osgar's neck.

*****

Cheska and Dr. Foehner sat among the Primes of the Aoratos and the small group of Metahumans.

"We have a lot to discuss today," Delfina said, "the first item, I'll address to Dr. Foehner."

Dr. Foehner was massaging a bandage over her bicep; the Aoratos had forcefully removed her beacon. She glanced at Delfina and nodded.

"You need to tell us why we shouldn't kill you," Delfina said. "Because of you, a Venator was able to find our Sanctuary, and, has very probably, killed Jakande."

"Del- " Dr. Foehner began.

"You'll address me as Prime, *Doctor* Foehner."

She nodded. "Prime, I had that beacon implanted years ago, when I became head of gravitics. I had forgotten about it. Besides, I don't even know how it's possible they tracked it down here. There's so much rock—it shouldn't have happened."

"Frankly, I don't really care about your motivations for not telling us. The simple fact is, you *cannot* be trusted. And we are a community that lives and dies on trust. That is our only shield against an enemy that is dominating all of humanity. Do you understand the scope of what we're facing here?" She let the question that settle over the assembled leaders like a frigid rain.

Dr. Foehner nodded.

Delfina continued, "We're not preserving a faction. Not a country. Not even a planet. We're trying to save the entire human race."

"Exactly how do you intend to do that, *Prime?*" Cheska spat her title in defiance. She was fed up with Delfina's withholding key information, and allowing Sat's murderer—and possibly Jak's, to live.

Delfina hadn't yet broken eye contact with Dr. Foehner. "We'll decide what to do with you later."

Dr. Foehner nodded in resignation.

She turned to Cheska. "I believe Jak mentioned the Prophecy of the Comps to you?"

"He did."

Delfina stood and paced back and forth along one side of the conference room. "Decades ago, one of our Metahuman descendants, Sibyl, had the gift of prescience—she was the first and only farseer. She predicted many things, all of which came true. Most of the time her gift allowed her to see an event days, maybe weeks in advance. In one case, she saw decades into the future. She predicted that two Abhumans would be born. These two Abhumans would know each other before ever meeting, would be able to sense each other from a great distance. They would be complementary Abhumans—comps."

Cheska was already starting to dislike the feel of this prophecy.

"The children of these comps," Delfina continued. "would inherit, not only their parents entire genetic memories, but their powers as well. Sibyl predicted that the children of the comps would be the downfall of the Covenant, and the liberators of humanity. Sadly, Sibyl was discovered and executed, but not before being tortured and her memories extracted. The Tarbizhad feared this Prophecy above all other threats. They went so far as to further manipulate the Artaldean faith, adding in myths about demons and possession, ensuring that any Abhumans would be discovered and turned in by their own people. Before The Prophecy, the Abhumans were just a nuisance, afterward, they were the ubiquitous boogeyman."

Cheska was waiting for the other shoe to drop, and she knew exactly where it was going to land.

Delfina locked eyes with Cheska. "You and Taro are the comps. That's why we gave you the only doses of the enhanced genome serum. If the comps can pass genetic memories on to their children, then your offspring are the future."

Cheska shook her head, disgusted. "I might only be sixteen-years-old, but I have the memories of an entire planet up here." She tapped her temple. "Bits of them, anyway. The Tarbizhad lied by virtue of implanting false memories in us. Vox Castus and the Confab lied to us. You lied to me—again and again. And you want me to trust you now? You've manipulated me every second I've been here. Why wouldn't you tell us about the prophecy before giving us the memory injection? Don't bother answering. I already know why. You wanted us to have no choice. You forced us into this. You're no better than the Tarbizhad."

Delfina leapt to her feet. "How dare you! You selfish little bitch." Delfina motioned to a mountainous guard named Titus. "Take her into custody. I can't trust her to do what's right for her own people." She motioned to

Taro. "Take him with her."

Cheska didn't resist, she just shook her head disapprovingly. When Titus escorted her in passed Delfina, Cheska said, "no different at all. Jak would be ashamed of you."

Delfina slapped Cheska hard across the face, leaving a red welt in the shape of her handprint. "Get her out of her."

Getting Loopy

THIS WOULD BE TAKE FOUR.

The last three times she'd looped back into the past, nothing she'd said to Delfina had worked. Would this time be any different? She had to try.

Cheska closed her eyes, allowing the kaleidoscope of space-time to blossom in her mind. Seeing into the past was the easiest—she already knew exactly what she'd done.

She returned, once again with Dr. Foehner, the Primes of the Aoratos and other Metahumans.

"We have a lot to discuss today," Delfina said, "the first item, I'll address to Dr. Foehner."

Yeah, Cheska thought, and this will be the fourth time we discuss it. Or rather, the fourth time I hear it.

Dr. Foehner was massaging a bandage over her

bicep; the Aoratos had forcefully removed her beacon. She glanced at Delfina and nodded.

Cheska leaned in toward Dr. Foehner and whispered, *"call her Prime. Trust me."*

"You need to tell us why we shouldn't kill you," Delfina said. "Because of you, a Venator assassin was able to find our Sanctuary, and, has very probably, killed Jakande."

"Prime-" Dr. Foehner began.

"At least she has the common sense to address me respectfully," Delfina said.

Dr. Foehner nodded. "Prime, I had that beacon implanted years ago, when I became head of gravitics. I had forgotten about it. Besides, I don't even know how it's possible they tracked it down here. There's so much rock—it shouldn't have happened."

"Frankly, I don't really care about your motivations for not telling us. The simple fact is, you cannot be trusted. And we are a community that lives and dies on trust. That is our only shield against an enemy that is dominating all of humanity. Do you understand the scope of what we're facing here?" She let that settle over the assembled leaders.

Dr. Foehner nodded.

Delfina continued, "we're not preserving a faction. Not a country. Not even a planet. We're trying to save the entire human race."

"Prime, might I ask how you intend to do that?" Cheska asked

Delfina hadn't yet broken eye contact with Dr. Foehner. "We'll decide what to do with you later."

Dr. Foehner nodded in resignation.

She turned to Cheska. "I believe Jak mentioned the Prophecy of the Comps to you?"

"He did."

Delfina stood and paced back and forth along one side of the conference room. "Decades ago, one of our Metahuman descendants, Sibyl, had the gift of prescience—she was the first and only farseer. She predicted many things, all of which came true. Most of the time her gift allowed her to see an event days, maybe weeks in advance. In one case, she saw decades into the future. She predicted that two Abhumans would be born—they were still using the term back then. These two Abhumans would know each other before ever meeting, would be able to sense each other from a great distance. They would be complementary Abhumans—comps."

"And," Cheska broke in, knowing exactly where this was going, "I'm guessing that these children would inherit all their parents's memories and powers?"

Delfina looked truly surprised and gave a single nod. "You have quite the capacity for deduction, Ms. Bellamy. And you are correct. Sibyl predicted that the children of the comps would be the downfall of the Covenant, and the liberators of humanity. Sadly, Sibyl was discovered and executed, but not before being tortured and her memories extracted. The Tarbizhad feared this Prophecy above all other threats. They went so far as to further manipulate the Artaldean faith, adding in myths about demons and possession, ensuring that any Abhumans would be discovered and turned in by their own people. Before the Prophecy, the Abhumans were just a nuisance, afterward, they were the ubiquitous boogeyman.”

“And,” Cheska interrupted again, “Taro and I are the comps.”

Delfina's face betrayed a hint of suspicion. She nodded.

“You gave Taro and me the serum so that you could ensure we did the right thing for our people,” Cheska said with an approving tone. “It makes sense.”

Now Delfina looked very surprised. “I'm glad to hear you approve.”

“Why wouldn't I? As you said, we *are* trying to save humanity. This is not about me, it's not about Taro, or even about you.”

Delfina smiled. “I underestimated you, Cheska.

“I might only be sixteen-years-old, but I have the memories of an entire planet up here.” She tapped her temple. “Bits of them, anyway. I understand what the Tarbizhad did. And that what you did, are doing, is the only way forward.”

Delfina strode to Cheska's seat and stood behind her, placing her hands on Cheska's shoulders. “This, my fellow Aoratos, is a wise young woman. We are blessed to have her in our circle.”

Cheers went up from around the table.

***

As they walked away from the conference room, Taro took Cheska's arm and whispered. “What was all that about?”

“What?” she asked.

"When did you become a fan of manipulation and lies?"

"Shh, quiet!" Cheska chided. "I'll explain when we're alone."

They found a quiet corner, and she told him.

"So Delfina is really no better than the Tarbizhad?" Taro concluded.

"In so far as lying, controlling people, and manipulating events? No. Though, she has humanity's best interests at heart. I believe that. But if we start discarding freedom, then how are we any better than the Tarbizhad?" Cheska asked.

"What will you do?"

"Me? What about we?"

"I meant we, I just mean- well, you seem to know what to do here."

Cheska smiled. "Thanks for the vote of confidence."

Taro stroked her arm. "I mean it, Cheska."

"I know you do. We have to be careful with Delfina. I used my bender powers to take a peek ahead at our meeting. I tried three different arguments with her. All failed. The only winning strategy was to agree with her, and pretend to be fully onboard. When I didn't, I ended up a prisoner. Literally. And so did you."

"So you're *not*? Onboard with her plan, that is?"

"How can I *not* be onboard with saving humanity?" Cheska threw up her arms.

"Yeah."

She nodded. "Yeah. She's a crazy woman, and I hate how she did what she did, on principle, but in practice … I don't know, Taro. Would we have done it differently?"

He shrugged.

"I'm trying not to be pissed at her. I'm really trying to see things from her perspective, but- I feel cheated. Violated. It's not that I hate the thought of having babies- "

"With me?" Taro asked, perking up.

Cheska twisted her mouth, making a funny face."I suppose. If you're my *comp*."

"Gee, thanks."

She sighed "I'm not ready to even think about babies, Taro. I know, I know, If I were still on *Ghimorphos*, then by next year I'd be expected to start trying. But I'm not—we're not—on *Ghimorphos*. We have a choice now. New options."

"But like you said, do we really?"

Cheska clenched her fists at her sides. "Argh! And that's what infuriates me! Because of an accident of birth, I have to:

a) have babies, and
b) save humanity?"

Taro threw his hands wide. "So what, then?"

"I'm trying to sort through all these memories, these feelings. I guess … I'm looking to our human past as a guide to our Metahuman future. I keep thinking about good versus evil. What defines that? The slave masters throughout history deprived slaves of free will, forcing them to do their bidding. That, to me, seems evil. What the Tarbizhad did to our people—evil. What Delfina did—is doing—is also depriving us of our freedom, but for a greater good. Does that make it *not* evil?"

"Dunno. I think you got all the philosopher memories," he cocked an eyebrow.

"We got the same memories."

He grinned. "But how would you know?"

"Can you be serious for a minute?"

"Sorry, just trying to lighten the mood."

"If we go along with this, our children would become these super-weapons. And we'd essentially have forced them into a fight they had no choice over. How is *that* not evil?"

"I get it," Taro said, "but what about this—any parent having a child is forcing that life to come into a world they didn't choose. Is that evil?"

"You're not helping." Cheska scowled. "But thanks for being serious."

"Who but the gods themselves are equipped to truly judge what is evil? I don't think I can answer the question. But, I do want to help free our people. Does that help you make a decision?"

Cheska nodded, but she wasn't sure she believed in the 'gods' part. There's always a choice. Between doing what's right, and not—the moral, versus the amoral. The good guys chose to do the right thing. Was the difference between good and evil simply failing to choose the moral option? And who designed that moral barometer?

***

Vox Castus had never journeyed to the Core. Then again, he'd never lost one of his Venators on a mission.

He knew *what* his masters were, but had never stood face-to-face with them in judgement. He decided to reject his fear. He shrugged it off, discarding it like an unwelcome garment in the heat of the day.

But fear was not so easy to leave behind.

The core of the *Ghimorphcs*—the Core, to the Artaldeans—was a place of great power, and the heart of the ship. It was an engine that birthed planets, and a weapon of terrible destruction; a fine balance of primal forces, like fire and ice. Where primal forces and humankind met, it did not go well for the frail human.

Castus contemplated his existence as his pod rocketed straight down the secret transit tube. Into the belly of the beast, he mused. The Tarbizhad had blessed each Vox—the Voces—with an awareness of the true nature of the Covenant. There were times that Castus wished he'd not been given such a *blessing*, for its knowledge was also a weighty burden. To be a frail creature, yet know the true nature of your existence, and still be powerless to rail against such forces … it could be a recipe for madness, and indeed, many were so driven.

His pod came to a stop and the door whisked open. He could feel the oppressive weight of gravity, dragging his limbs down, slowing his every step, as he rose to exit.

He stood in a great cave. It was a warren of tunnels unlike any man made structure, its ambiance, more organic. It was a place of darkness, only the dimmest glow of scattered bioluminescent fungi tolerated for the Tarbizhad's servants. The place smelled of death, of rot. Damp, moist, and heavy, hung the scent of decay in the fetid air.

A dim path of glowing red, snaked along the floors. At seemingly random places, tunnel entrances or exits pierced the walls. Castus swallowed hard and continued down the red path. It led out of the cave and into a smaller chamber. He continued for long minutes, winding ever deeper into the maze of the Core.

The path terminated in a great cylindrical room. It seemed to reach up to infinity. It too, was perforated with tunnels, many of them soaring above him. There were no stairs, or ladders, or handholds. How any creature could possibly reach those tunnels was a mystery to Castus. He felt his body lighten drastically, almost back to what he'd call normal.

"*Report,*" came a voice. No, not a voice, Castus realized, a thought?

Castus bowed his head reverently. "Master."

"*You may call me, First,*" it thought to him.

Castus still saw nothing or nobody. His eyes darted around the dark cylinder. A silo perhaps? "First, I have come as you requested."

"*You lost your hunter.*"

"Yes, First. Not lost- exactly, but he has failed to report in," Castus said.

"*You lost your hunter,*" the First repeated.

"Yes, First. Venator Osgar's signal has been lost, and he is two days overdue to report back."

"*And why do you think that is?*" the First thought to him.

Castus felt a presence, perhaps behind him. His skin crawled as he tried to formulate an answer while holding back the panic he felt boiling in his guts. "The

Abhuman had help."

"Indeed," the First said aloud, in a creaking, ticking baritone. Castus shuddered at the sound and swallowed.

"I believe there was more than one Abhuman," Castus managed.

Without a sound, a great, pale humanoid appeared out of the shadows to the right of Castus. He resisted fearfully spinning to meet the creature, instead, slowly turning to meet his master's gaze. That proved impossible, for his master had no eyes. Nor ears.

The First stood several heads taller than Castus and wore skin as pale blue as moonlight. His? Its- head was oversized, as if its brain had stretched beyond the confines of a normal skull. Its limbs were long and gangly, bending at odd angles, but looked ever so dangerous.

The First clicked and ticked as it crawled on all fours, slowly, around Castus. He swore the creature tasted the air, for he spotted a long, pink tongue flick out of its mouth. Castus realized he was trembling and cursed his weakness, willing his body to stillness.

"More than one, you say?" the First said.

"Yes, First. I believe so."

"That is rare."

The First was still circling Castus when he caught sight of something in the shadows at the First's feet. The First was dragging something—someone! Castus swallowed the terror that rose in this throat and threatened to paint the floor with his vomit.

The First held up the mangled human corpse. "You came at mealtime," the First said, taking a bite of the man? Woman? Castus could no longer tell. The First's fangs must have been a foot long.

"How will you rectify this situation, Vox Castus?"

Hearing his name—in that voice, sent waves of ice through his veins. He felt his fingers numbing. "I believe we need to assemble a group of Watchers to accompany a second Venator. I will send them back down to the planet and track down this, or *these*, Abhumans." His words contained much more conviction than he felt.

Several shadows moved, and Castus caught glints of light reflected off skin. Five naked Artaldeans filed into the cylindrical chamber from a ground level entrance.

"Do not mind me, Vox Castus, my second course is here." The First moved like an exploding shadow, straight to an Artaldean woman, punching a hole through her stomach with an outstretched limb, more weapon than hand. She dropped to the floor. The other four scattered, trying to run back out of the tunnel they'd come in. A hatch slid down with an echoing *clunk*. They pounded at the hatch for a moment, then scattered as the First roared at them, galloping on all fours like a beast. He leapt impossibly high, like a mutant lion. This creature made mockery of the human form—of the Artaldeans.

The First cleaved and rent, gutted and mutilated their flesh. Castus stood, corpse-still, breathing in shallow gasps, as limbs and gore flew about the creature's lair. He ate them—all of them.

When the First was finished with his meal, he stood on his hind legs, as if affecting manhood. He rose to nearly three-meters in height, Castus guessed, then strode to the Vox, wiping gore from his thin lips, exposing the great fangs which gleamed like white daggers.

"I will go to Krijese and rectify this problem," the First said. Castus watched a bulge in the First's belly, rippling like a snake digesting its prey. "I tolerate one mistake only, Vox Castus."

For a split second he wondered what would happen if he made a second, then needed no answer as he remembered the carnage.

The First's lips curled up, as if smiling. "Leave. Now."

Before Castus could turn, the First exploded upward, like a shaft of darkness and shadow, soaring up the great cylinder to impossible heights. Then, he was gone.

Castus flinched at the sound of the lower hatches sliding open. It took every part of him not to run screaming from that den of horrors—from the Core.

Training Day

CHESKA AND HER NEW ABHUMAN friends stood in the gymnasium. Each wore a suit of flat-black, semi-rigid scout armor, with full-face helmets and integral atmospheric systems. In addition to their sidearms and knives, they carried heavy plasma rifles. They were lined up before the head of the resistance, Delfina Cifuentes. Cheska felt the tingling recognition near all her Abhuman allies. It was an interesting feeling. She'd have to ask Delfina about it.

"Team," Delfina said, "Meet Cheska. Cheska, meet the team."

Cheska walked down the line of four Metahumans, not including Delfina and Taro.

"Rupinder you have already met," Delfina said.

Cheska nodded and shook his hand. *What was his*

power, she wondered.

"He's the Military Prime and chief tactical instructor."

They moved down to Zula. "Zula is our Technology Prime, and I believe you've seen her cybernetic powers in action."

"I have," Cheska said. Cyber for the win.

"Glad your sticking around," Zula said.

"Thanks."

Next in line was an enormous, swarthy man, maybe of Greek descent? Cheska remembered him. He was the man who'd taken her into custody on Delfina's orders—no, that had been another version of time, or rather, had never been at all. It had simply been one permutation of an infinite number of futures. She knew he was the Aoratos Security Prime, responsible for the local police force—like the Watchers on the *Ghimorphos* … or, maybe not.

"Titus Sinclair," he said, shaking her hand.

As she shook his hand it seemed to dissolve like mist. She yanked her hand back sharply.

He smiled. "I'm a stoneskin."

"Stoneskin?" Cheska asked.

"I can control my body density." He proffered a hand again. "Squeeze."

Cheska did—it was hard as stone this time.

She walked to the fourth, and last, Metahuman—a very attractive woman in her twenties, with long, wavy auburn hair and piercing blue eyes. They were magnetic. Cheska had a hard time looking away. Cheska liked boys, but even so, she found this woman attractive in ways she didn't think she should.

"Felicia Raines," she said, shaking Cheska's hand, who hadn't even remembered extending it.

"Cheska Bellamy."

Felicia smiled. "Yes, we all know who you are, dear heart."

"What- can you do?" Cheska managed to ask.

"Oh, where do I start?" she said with a mischievous grin. "Only teasing."

Cheska giggled like she was five.

"I'm a teep. I can read minds," Felicia whispered, leaning close to Cheska's face, "peer into your deepest, darkest secrets." She leaned back and smiled. "Comes in very handy in my line of work."

"Oh?" Cheska said, genuinely curious.

"Intel, dear heart, getting to the truth. I'm the Aoratos Intelligence Prime."

Cheska swore this woman was a hypnotist.

"Go easy, Felicia. I didn't bring Cheska here for you to flirt with her," Delfina said.

"Of course not. But since she's here ..." Felicia batted her eyelashes at Cheska, then laughed.

Cheska walked back to stand beside Taro, who elbowed her gently. "Hey, I saw how you were looking at Felicia. I'm jealous."

"*Shut up!*," Cheska whispered, scowling.

"That is the team," Delfina said to Cheska. "Though you've met Rupinder before, I don't think you've seen what he can do—outside of his myriad martial accomplishments that is."

Cheska shook her head.

Delfina nodded to Rupinder. He took a deep breath and began to chant.

"*Ohmmmm, Ohmmmmmm, Ohmmmm, Ohmmmmmmm.*" The floor began to shake, Cheska's head buzzed, limbs trembled, the waves of his voice suffusing her body … Rupinder stopped abruptly.

"He's what we call a hardsinger," Delfina said.

"Wow. Loud!" Cheska said.

"Sadly, with the loss of Saturnalia," Delfina continued, "we six are the only free Abhumans known to the Aoratos. My hope is that each of us can learn to work together as a team, using our powers to help liberate our people as an end goal. This won't happen overnight. Six of us can't hope to wage war against the Tarbizhad, but we can work together to free other Abhumans, grow the resistance. This is a long game we're playing here, folks. A marathon, if you will, not a sprint.

And so they began.

***

Cheska made her daily trip to the infirmary to look in on Jak. For days he'd been unconscious, ever closer to death. She'd even entertained trying to skip back in time to save him, and managed to make several consecutive jumps of a minute each back into the past, but it was so taxing, and after ten quick jumps, taking her ten-minutes into the past, she'd collapsed from exhaustion and had an uncontrollable nose-bleed, so bad, she'd had to call Taro to heal her. She wouldn't be able to save Jak.

She stood over him as he lay on his bed. She stroked

his tight curly hair, wishing she'd told him how much she loved him. She'd never loved anyone beside her mother and father, and her mother might be lost to her now. Taro was certainly becoming important to her, but there was nobody like Jak. He was part brother, part father.

She held back the tears. She hadn't the first couple of days, but she was learning to deal with the grief. She might never see her mother again, but she wasn't dead. She could cling to a thread of hope that she might rescue her, and in that hope she kept grief at bay. But Jak? If he was dying, then she'd have to deal with that. She couldn't pretend it wasn't happening. Though that's exactly what she wanted to do.

She held his hand, felt the warmth still in his body, and the former strength that had protected her for two years. He'd been her guardian angel. She was glad she had the right metaphor for him now. Watcher was a fine title, but he truly had been like an angel.

"I love you, old man. I- I'm sorry … I never told you."

Cheska felt him squeeze her hand. She gasped.

"*You just did*," Jak croaked. Jak's eyes fluttered open and he took a breath then smacked his lips.

Wiping tears from her stinging eyes, Cheska asked, "You want water?"

"Got something stronger?" He smirked.

***

The next day Jak was up and around, dressed and walking. Cheska and Delfina were both in his room at the infirmary.

"How is this possible?" Cheska asked Dr. Mavros.

"Our friend Jak isn't exactly normal," he said.

Cheska shook her head. "What do you mean?"

"I'm an Abhuman, kiddo. Like you," Jak said.

Cheska turned to Delfine. "Why didn't you tell me?"

"Jak wanted to tell you himself."

Cheska turned back to Jak. "What? But how?"

"Same as you. Born to it."

"But, how come I don't sense a tingling around you? Every time I meet an Abhuman, I get this weird feeling all over my body. Like static electricity or something."

Jak put a huge hand on her shoulder. Cheska could feel the strength back in his limbs. "Think back to when we first met. Two years ago."

She tried.

"You were drawn to me. I remember you saying so," Jak said.

"Yeah, I remember now. There *might* have been a tingling. Why not now?"

Delfina stepped close to Cheska. "Our benefactors built in this recognition sense for Abhumans. This tingling—as you describe it—is like two opposing magnets coming close—they're drawn together. But this sense works more like smell. You know that if you live with a scent every day, you become accustomed to it, and eventually forget about it. A new person coming into your home might notice, or you might, after a long absence, but otherwise it's invisible to you. It works like that. You and Jak are just accustomed to each other, and you were so young when you first met, it wasn't obvious to you back then."

"So, your power is healing?" Cheska asked.

"Sort of. Part of it anyway. My mutations is a little different. Instead of one main power, I have a few smaller ones. I can heal, but nothing like Taro. I'm a bit stronger than most humans, and a bit faster. I was meant to watch out for people. I'm a sentinel."

"Wow," Cheska said, at a loss for words.

"But the important question is," Jak said, "how do I smell?"

Cheska punched him in the shoulder, as she loved to do. And as usual, she tweaked her wrist, though not as much this time—pushups were definitely helping.

***

Cheska sat cross-legged on her pillow while Taro lay on his back, draped across the end of her bed, his legs dangling off the edge, his hands behind his head.

They'd been sitting quietly for a long while, then Cheska spoke, "How do I tell Jak about Delfina?"

"Tell him what, exactly?" Taro asked.

"Oh, that his long-lost partner is a crazy lady? That she would have locked you and me up if I hadn't gone along with her plan?"

Taro sat up on one elbow. "Cheska, that never happened- not exactly."

Cheska threw up her hands, face clenched. "Damn you, Taro, it did happen!" She softened slightly. "Or at least it *could* have happened. She's capable of it."

"Right. We're all capable of terrible things. That doesn't mean that we will do those things. Agree?"

Cheska shrugged, looking sullen. "I can't trust her."

"I'm not asking you to. I'm simply saying that you

can't convict someone of what they're capable of. That's madness."

"So, I'm crazy now?"

"C'mon, you know that's not what I meant." Taro placed a hand on her knee, but she returned the gesture with a scowl.

"I need to do something" Cheska said. She was so angry. She felt powerless, more so than at any other time in her life.

Maybe she could do something about that …

***

Delfina looked back at Cheska incredulously. "You want to lead a raid against the terraforming infrastructure?"

Cheska nodded solemnly. "Somewhere close to where the Indigens are hiding. I want them to see us acting against the terraforming. Then maybe they'll see us as possible allies. You said that Taro and I are the keys to the future. Well, it's time we started taking that responsibility seriously. We can't hide here inside Sanctuary while the Indigens die, and while the Tarbizhad and our own people make plans to kill us. More will come for us—surely you realize that?"

"We've survived here for decades by being cautious. Destroying a random terraforming factory in itself is reasonable, but one near where the Indigens are hiding? Foolish. Our people are watching for Indigens. At best, you'll expose these innocent creatures, already barely surviving. Worst case, you get them and yourselves killed. You and Taro are too important to the future of humanity to risk on such a mission."

Cheska's temper was in full solar-flare mode now.

"Then why the hell did you bother giving us weapons and combat training? I thought you wanted to tap into our powers to fight back?"

"I wanted to prepare you in case the worst happened —like if someone broke into the facility and you were forced to defend yourself?" The assassin, Cheska realized. Once again, Delfina was right. "Surely you'd agree that I was right to prepare you? I believe you'd be dead right now if not for Rupinder's lessons. I will not sanction you leaving on a mission outside Sanctuary. That's my final word on the matter."

We'll see about that, Cheska thought.

She looped back *eight times*, trying different arguments with Delfina, all with the same result—what a stubborn old bitch!

Cheska looped back to when she'd received Delfina's answer. "Well, I had to try," Cheska said. "I understand your position. Thanks for taking me seriously."

"Thank you for understanding. Frankly I'm impressed with the maturity I see here. I've got high hopes for you, Cheska."

Cheska forced a smile.

She was getting much better at lying.

She was learning.

***

Two black shapes slipped between shadows, oozing like liquid mercury. Cheska and Taro, clad in their scout armor, and carrying their full load-out of weapons, skulked through the compound.

They huddled against the stone walls before the blast doors, waiting for the great slabs to rumble open. Taro

136

was in the lead, Cheska crouched behind him, her hand on his shoulder. A deep vibration suffused their legs as the doors began to slowly creak open. An Aoratos long-range patrol was returning to base.

Once the patrol marched past, they waited until the doors began to close again and slipped through.

Taro led Cheska into one of the small vehicle bays at the base of the great cone-shaped cavern. Taro threw a leg over a long tube, that looked pretty much like a probe. Cheska remembered something called a torpedo, and something called a motorcycle, which seemed to be the parents of this contraption. Cheska could feel waves of heat emanating from the vehicle. It must have been one the patrol had just returned on.

After Taro had disabled the alarm, he said, "Get on."

"Are you sure it will take two of us?" she asked.

"Positive. I've flown a gravbike before." He proffered a hand to her. Cheska took it and Taro pulled her aboard.

The engine, already warm, spooled up almost instantaneously, and she felt an energy field surround them—like static electricity—shimmering all around them.

The gravbike lifted gently off the floor of the cave and Cheska felt a welt on the seat rise up behind her, cupping her buttocks. Straps extruded from the seat and clamped her legs down. Taro must have felt Cheska flinch.

"It's ok, just the safety harness. So you don't fall off," he said. The gravbike slipped gently forward toward the center of the great cavern.

"Why would I fall off? It seems pretty stable?"

Taro turned back and grinned.

Cheska's eyes went wide as two moons as the gravbike's nose jerked upward, the vehicle exploding up the shaft of the cavern, up to a dim flicker of light.

***

The gravbike soared a thousand meters above the surface of Krijese. Slipping silently above the rust-colored planet, made black by night. Just a tiny hint of blood-red reflected from the moon which the Artaldean's had pulled into orbit.

"It's peaceful up here," Cheska said.

"Yeah, it sure is."

Cheska had her arms around Taro—ostensibly to hold on—but it felt good.

A beeping sounded from the gravbike controls and a light flashed. Taro's head whipped toward the signal.

"What is it?" Cheska asked.

"We've got company!" he said, glancing behind them.

"Delfina?"

"Probably. Somebody must have noticed the gravbike missing. Or, maybe I'm not as good at hacking alarms as I thought I was?"

Four gravbikes formed up beside Cheska and Taro, two on each side, each had one rider. They matched speed and altitude, but didn't make any aggressive motions.

"Where do you think you're going?" Felicia asked, her voice coming through the gravbike's comm system.

"To do something," Cheska replied.
"Without your team mates?" Felicia asked.
Cheska smiled.

Synergy

<hr>

SIX METAHUMANS ON A MISSION. Cheska finally felt like they were accomplishing something. And judging by the fact that the other four Metahumans had joined her, they must feel the same way. Maybe they had concerns with Delfina as well?

They'd flown three hours southwest at the gravbike's top speed of 740 kph. That took them just over 2,000 kilometers away from Sanctuary, and hopefully, far enough that they wouldn't be traced back.

"There it is, four clicks out," Rupinder informed them over comms.

Cheska peered over Taro's shoulder, and sure enough, saw the target lit up on the gravbike's HUD, which was projected onto the inner-surface of the shielding.

"What's the plan again?" Cheska asked.

Taro put a hand on her knee. "The gravbikes are equipped with dual plasma rifles. And before you ask, yes, the same ones we carry. But, plugged into the gravbikes, they tap into the bike's power plant and can fire much hotter bolts, and more of them."

"No danger of the emitters burning out?" Cheska asked, still unconvinced.

"Nah, they're designed to handle them. Being in the Aoratos is all about maximizing use of scarce materials. We can't afford to have twenty different types of weapons."

They were closing on the terraforming plant at an alarming rate, and descending as well. The plant itself resembled what Cheska now remembered as an old Earth nuclear power plant's cooling tower—though instead of conducting heat upward, this plant belched out endless clouds of the gasses required to make Krijese's atmosphere breathable to Artaldeans—humans, she corrected herself.

The plant had been built over an open fault in the planetary crust, and tapped into the vast geothermal energy to power its systems. Upthrust sheets of cooled magma littered the landscape around the terraforming plant.

"Here we go!" Taro said. "We'll fire a few volleys, knock out the power, then go in and sabotage things permanently. We'll make sure these plants never operate again."

Cheska didn't respond, she just clung to Taro like a baby chimpanzee to its mother. An apt simile now that she had the image of them in her memory.

The five gravbikes dove at the terraforming plant like birds of prey. A barrage of purple flashes preceded the shrill screech of plasma bolts, stitching streaks of fire onto the tall structure.

The gravbikes all banked away hard, the straps over Cheska's legs dug into her thighs and the seat into her lower back. She closed her eyes and clenched her jaw. Then the g-force abated. She opened her eyes to see the gravbike descending at a much more prosaic pace. The terraforming plant's toxic effluence now ebbed.

"You ok?" Taro asked.

Cheska nodded, but of course he couldn't see that. "Yep. I'll live. I think."

The gravbikes all touched down gently and her teammates dismounted. All wore the black scout suits and were fully armed, toting extra power packs for their plasma rifles and pistols.

"What now?" Cheska said to the group over comms.

Rupinder held up a flexible bundle of green tubes. "Nano-corrosives. When these charges blow, the nanites will spread through the structure like a disease. We'll make sure we salvage anything useful first, of course."

"Are any of our people in there?" Cheska asked.

"Our people?" Felicia asked.

"You know what I mean, Artaldeans."

"There might be," Titus said, taking the lead.

The team crept up on the battered terraforming plant, smoke billowing from the holes where the plasma shots had bored through its outer shell. Titus led them to a staircase leading up the side of the building.

Cheska's suit amplified a click, like a door opening. Titus held up a closed fist—the team halted. The door at the top of the staircase opened a crack.

"**Artaldean engineers**," Titus boomed, in a voice augmented by his suit, "**we will allow you safe passage away from the facility We are here to destroy the factory, not harm Artaldeans. You have thirty-seconds to comply.**"

The door clicked shut and Cheska watched the timer countdown on her helmet's HUD.

At eighteen-seconds remaining, the door opened again and Cheska saw an arm toss something.

"Grenade!" Titus yelled, then ran toward the thrown object.

"What's he doing!" Cheska screamed.

"His job," Taro said, yanking her arm. "Trust him."

The five remaining Metahumans dove to the ground, minimizing their exposed area, hands over their heads. Our of the corner of Cheska's eye, she spotted Titus. For a micro-second his entire body, armor and all, shifted color, turning a milky prismatic color. The grenade exploded with a flash of blue light and a minor concussive charge, all of which Titus's body deflected away from the team.

"EMP grenade," Rupinder said.

The other Metahumans stood. Cheska was shocked to see that Titus seemed entirely unharmed. She knew on an intellectual level that he could control his body's density, but she hadn't realized that extended to his armor and equipment as well, which also appeared pristine.

"Guess they don't want to come out nicely?" Taro said.

"No, they seem to like it in there," Titus said. "Rupinder, you think you could persuade them to come out?"

"It would be my pleasure," Rupinder said, with a sweeping bow.

Titus nodded. "The rest of you, stay behind Rupinder till he clears the room. Got it?" Titus bounded up the stairs, two at a time. He tried the door first—locked. His right gauntlet shimmered, as his body had before. Like diamond, Cheska mused. He slammed the prismatic hand into the spot on the door where the locking mechanism had been. Presently there was a ragged hole of twisted metal. Titus's entire body phased again and he opened the door.

The big man was met with a barrage of plasma pistol fire—small bolts and short bursts. He stood like a human shield as the engineers fired on him. His body just seemed to soak it all up, or maybe deflect it, Cheska wasn't quite sure which. They all seemed to burn through their power cartridges at the same time, which was what Titus had apparently been waiting for.

Titus stepped sideways suddenly and Rupinder leapt f o r w a r d ,   b e l l o w i n g. "*Ahhhhhhhhhhhhhhhhhhhhhhhhhhhhhhhhhhhhh!*"

Cheska was sure she could see a cone of sound erupt from Rupinder. Maybe it was just the secondary effects on dust particles—regardless, it was awesome to behold. The engineers, she counted four, all fell to their knees, clutching their helmets. In less than two-seconds they had all collapsed.

Titus jumped in front of Rupinder again, sweeping his plasma rifle across the room, looking for additional threats. When he found none, he motioned for the rest of the team to come in.

The engineers were promptly disarmed and secured outside of the facility. The team wasn't able to find much of use, but what they did find was stripped and loaded on the gravbikes.

"Not bad for your first mission," Taro said to Cheska.

"Well, I didn't do much," she said.

"Nor were you supposed to. It's a team. I don't shoot things unless I have to. I heal. That's my role."

"What *is* my role, then?" Cheska asked, sincerely curious, because she didn't know.

"I guess we're still figuring that part out."

"Contacts!" Felicia shouted.

"Where?" Titus asked.

"Coming in from the east, 0.5 clicks out, vectoring to us at … 4 kph?" Felicia said, looking confused.

Cheska looked up to the eastern sky but saw nothing. If ships were that close, then she'd expect to see them, even small gravbikes.

Then Cheska spotted them.

***

They came as shimmering outlines in the distance. Not corporeal, per se, more like sketches of something. The creatures were tall and had elongated heads, but it was the legs that cinched it for Cheska—she'd only ever seen

145

two creatures with legs that bent backward at the knee, instead of forward.

"Hold your fire!" Cheska shouted. "It's them."

"Them who?" Felicia asked.

"The Indigens. Don't shoot!" Cheska pleaded.

"Stand down," Titus commanded.

Seven shimmering outlines coalesced into solid humanoids as they approached—as if they'd turned off some kind of stealth or cloaking system. They formed a semi-circle in front of the Metahumans, weapons trained on them, though not making any overtly aggressive movements.

"Now what?" Taro asked Cheska on a private channel.

"We talk to them," she replied to the group. "Felicia, have we ever tried telepathy with them?"

"No. I'm the first telepath in decades. We're rare, apparently."

Cheska nodded. "Well then, I guess this is our opportunity. Like a first contact."

Felicia nodded.

"Just- " Cheska started, "just try to communicate to them. Let them know we mean them no harm." Cheska tapped her breastplate then pointed to the engineers tied up outside the facility.

The Indigen made some kind of hissing noise when they saw the engineers in the bright-yellow terraforming suits.

"Cheska, take off your gauntlet and give me your hand," Felicia said.

Cheska didn't even question it. The atmosphere

wouldn't hurt her skin, not in the short term, anyway. She slipped her gauntlet off and held out a hand to Felicia, who took it gently. Immediately Cheska felt a surge in her mind—like she'd drank an entire pot of coffee.

"Sorry, forgot to warn you. It can be a bit intense at first," Felicia thought to her. "We'll talk to our new friends together."

"Can I talk to them?" Cheska thought to Felicia.

"Anytime. Just focus on him and start talking. He'll hear it inside his mind, and hopefully, you'll hear what he says."

One of the Indigens seemed to be the leader of the seven. At least that was Cheska's assumption. *It* had moved itself forward. Did they have gender?

"Greetings, my name is Cheska Bellamy. We hope to work peacefully with you," she said.

The creature made some kind of grunting noise, but otherwise didn't say anything.

Cheska took a breath and summoned an extra measure of courage. "I'm terribly sorry for what happened to your planet. We did not know you were here."

"It speaks lies," the creature finally said. Or rather, said something which Cheska heard, but then she understood the intent inside her mind.

"No." Shit. He was right, of course. The Artaldeans had known the Indigens were here. "These people," she pointed to the bound engineers, "*not* our people."

"It lies. Looks the same. One people," it said.

How did you explain to an alien species that your

own people had lied to you, wiped your memories, created a fake religion, and generally deluded you for centuries? Cheska thought these stilted exchanges would somehow fall short. She'd hoped mind-to-mind communication would make things clear, but then, she supposed, these creatures must think quite differently. Cheska pointed up to the sky. "Bad creatures brought us here. Made us hurt your planet." She let that hang for a moment.

As if Cheska had called down the wrath of the gods, green bolts of energy slammed into the ground, entirely vaporizing the rearmost Indigen. Something huge and fast flashed over head, obscuring the remainder of the dim moonlight for an instant.

"Scatter!" Titus roared.

The team bolted in random directions, looking for what little cover they could find. The Indigens began firing on the Metahumans.

Cheska had ducked behind a sheet of cooled lava and Taro had followed her. "They think we're responsible!" Cheska wailed.

"Nothing we can do about it now except survive. Understand me?" Taro said in a commanding tone.

She nodded and locked the gauntlet back onto her suit.

"You stay close to me, ok?" he said.

"I will," Cheska said, knowing that she might not be able to.

"Titus," Taro said over comms, "who is it?"

"Not sure. A single ship. Never see its type before. Damned powerful cannons though. I'd like those on my gravbike," Titus said.

"Maybe we can ask them for a set?" Felicia said sarcastically.

"It's coming back for another pass! Heads down!" Titus said.

A barrage of fluorescent-green bolts slammed into the ground, vaporizing frozen moisture and causing the ground to explode in pockets—Cheska understood the physics well, but to see this principle in action was frightful.

The Metahumans opened fire, an orange firestorm erupting from the ground.

One of the Indigens had moved out from behind cover and began shooting up at the craft. Cheska caught a good look at it. It was sleek and black, tentacles drifting behind it, like a squid from Earth's oceans. Its maw vomited fluorescent-green death and vaporized a second of the Indigens, though the return fire from her team and the Indigens seemed to have damaged the craft and Cheska saw it trailing smoke as it banked off.

The remaining Indigens loped after the craft as it descended, appearing to be headed for a crash. Their gait was extraordinary—their reverse knees and longer legs gave them a tremendous bounding stride. They ran at least three time as fast as any human, according to the stats her suit provided.

"Follow them!" Titus commanded.

The Indigens seemed to be more focused on this new threat for the moment, and had suspended firing at the Metahumans. Maybe a common enemy could bind them together? The ship slammed into the brittle basalt, ejecting a mass of shards around its point of impact.

The Indigens surrounded the crashed ship, their weapons trained on the wreckage. The Metahumans were close behind.

When Cheska arrived at the crashed ship, she was surprised to find it mostly intact. That was an incredibly resilient machine. One of the Indigens stepped into the edges of the shallow impact crater, his weapon leading. He prodded what might have been the canopy of the ship.

"Looks like a fighter," Zula said. "Not one I've seen before."

"You mean we have ships like this?" Cheska asked, shocked.

"Of course they do. They have lots of secrets, little girl," Zula said.

The canopy jerked open a crack. A pale, grey hand —claw—emerged, probing. The Indigen jabbed at the hand with his rifle and was rewarded with a burst of red mist that coated his faceplate. He jumped back, but seemed uninjured.

A fist erupted from the canopy, smashing through the material. A muscular shadow bolted upward, barely registering in Cheska's vision.

"Where did it go?" Titus said.

Cheska knew what this was. It was one of *them*—the Tarbizhad.

***

Cheska stopped thinking. It was time do. She stood tall

and projected her will forcefully outward, imagining a great sphere of time, freezing all in its path. Sure enough, they froze, mid movement. She glanced around, looking for the Tarbizhad—he was here, somewhere.

A wave of nausea pounded her belly. Realizing it wasn't just nerves, she focused on it, used it. The feeling of nausea was coming *from* somewhere. She could sense the creature! It was the source of that feeling. She spun.

It was crawling through the air in mid-flight, not quite frozen as the rest of them were. It was several meters above them and on a downward trajectory, straight for—Taro! I

The Tarbizhad seemed to be speeding up, despite Cheska exerting her will ever more forcefully. It was as if the Tarbizhad was fighting her power. She took three steps and shoved Taro out of the way, unslinging her rifle. She stepped to the side as the Tarbizhad descended to where Taro would have been.

Cheska opened fire.

The flow of time exploded back into being, as if a stream had been undammed. From an almost peaceful state, the world around Cheska erupted in chaos.

The Tarbizhad howled as Cheska's plasma rifle burned into its flesh. It missed its intended victim, slamming into the basalt. In the time it took to scream, the beast had burst upward again in a flash of shadow.

Gods above! What was this?

Titus grabbed Cheska and Taro. "Stay with me! Guard them with your lives!" Titus roared at the team. The rest of the Metahumans closed in around Cheska and Taro.

No! She didn't want them to sacrifice themselves for her. It was her turn to help. She froze time again, if only for a heartbeat, and slipped through the ring of bodies.

The Tarbizhad, likely sensing easier prey, had landed on one of the Indigens. Finally Cheska saw the monster in its fully horror. Though hunched over its victim, she knew it must stand three meters tall, at least. Its gangly limbs were covered in translucent, mottled white skin, under which, black sparks erupted here and there. Even though she could see it now, there was still an aura of shadow about it. Like wisps of the blackest smoke.

Cheska fired her rifle again before time resumed its normal flow. She got another full burst off before the creature once again leapt up into the sky.

"Cheska!" Titus roared. "Damn you, girl!" He dashed over to her but stopped abruptly when he saw the mangled corpse of the Indigen. The remaining five Indigens stood in shock, all the fight seemed drained from them.

"Where is it?" Rupinder asked. "Anyone have eyes on the damned thing?"

The team all trained their weapons outward, away from Cheska, again providing a virtual shield. A flash of white and red appeared, and Zula screamed, clutching her face-mask, clawing at it. She fell to her knees. Taro moved to her as the rest of them closed ranks.

Cheska glanced down at the Zula's beautiful ebony skin, now covered with writhing bloody tendrils, not on her skin, but under. Taro pulled off her gauntlets and held her hand, focusing on her. Zula's eyes grew wide, then went still. Her whole body went still.

Taro looked up to Cheska and shook his head.

Cheska stood, all fear erased. She was enraged. "Listen to me!" she yelled. "Stop trying to protect me, and work with me. We can kill this thing, but *only* if we work together."

She could see the fear in their eyes as they glanced back at her. Titus nodded and Rupinder moved aside to let her pass. She could do this. She had to do this.

"Rupinder, make some noise!" Cheska said.

Rupinder lifted his face to the sky and bellowed, "Rrrrrooooooooooooooowwww!"

Cheska caught a shimmer, just the briefest disturbance. She projected a mental bubble of time outward, away from the team, and they all watched in amazement as the Tarbizhad hung frozen in the sky above them. Up and down seemed to have no meaning to this creature. It was like the Tarbizhad swam in three dimensions, as if air were water.

"Fire!" Titus commanded.

The entire team, and the Indigens, opened up with everything they had. A torrent of energy struck the Tarbizhad, riddling its body with burns, flesh melting off it as Cheska held it hanging frozen in time.

"Can't- hold- it- much- longer!" She gasped. Her time bubble collapsed and the creature pounced on the circle of Metahumans.

It roared.

A sound slammed into Cheska's body like a falling building. It was something between the screech of a bat and the trumpet of an elephant. A sound that embodied every wicked act and deed that had ever been thought or done—a sound that Cheska would never forget.

It was overwhelming.

The Metahumans fell to their knees, powerless in the face of this ultimate evil.

The Tarbizhad swung its clawed hand like a great scythe, tearing through Titus's armor and flesh, toppling Rupinder, and sending Felicia rolling backward. Once again, it exploded up into the night, vanishing.

Felicia picked herself up. "Back to the terraforming plant! Inside!" she commanded.

"We are *not* prepared for this, Felicia," Taro said.

She spun on him. "You think I don't get that? Help your team mates."

Rupinder was able to hobble back to the terraforming building himself, but it took the remaining three to drag Titus into the building. The Indigens had scattered.

"Bar that door, Rupinder!" Felicia said.

Taro already had his hands on Titus's stomach and Cheska could see the big man's flesh knitting before her eyes. Titus groaned, which was good, that meant he was alive.

"You going to be all right, tough guy?" Felicia asked Titus.

Titus smiled. "Hope so. Who's going to keep you in line, woman?"

Cheska thought she saw the barest hint of a tear in

Felicia's eye. That was more than concern for a team mate. Felicia said nothing and turned back to the door.

"Secure?" Felicia asked Rupinder.

"As much as it can be. At least we know where that thing will be coming in," Rupinder said.

"What's the plan, Felicia? Are we just going to hide in here? If that was a Tarbizhad, then he, it—whatever —knows exactly where we are." Then it occurred to Cheska that it was strange that such a being would come alone. "Surely it has back up on the way?"

"Maybe," Felicia said. "But if we go back out there, we're dead. You saw what that thing is capable of? It moves like light-speed."

"Then we don't go out," Cheska explained. "But we open the door."

"Set a trap?" Rupinder asked.

Cheska nodded. "Exactly. And we need to hurry up. If it's not alone, then we need to kill it fast.

And so, they made a plan.

***

"Everyone in position?" Cheska asked.

The team nodded.

Titus was fully healed thanks to Taro, but was very fatigued after his efforts. The team had great powers, but they weren't limitless; they were like batteries, and even batteries needed to recharge. Use them too much, and they could burn out, or worse, explode.

Cheska nodded to Rupinder, who opened the door.

Titus stood in the shadows, just beyond the open door, and directly in front of the other team members.

"I can feel it," Cheska shouted. "It's coming." She

155

had a feeling almost the opposite of what she experienced near other Metahumans—instead of a pleasant tingling, she got an overwhelming feeling of dread—a cold uneasiness. Cheska felt it flying at the open door.

"Now!"

Titus shimmered, his suit glistened beautifully, then turned clear as glass.

Titus braced and grabbed the Tarbizhad as it slammed into him. Cheska felt the impact of the Tarbizhad on Titus's impenetrable body. Ripples of energy from the collision suffused the building.

Cheska slowed time—she didn't have strength left to freeze it. The team began to fire at the Tarbizhad's limbs, Titus being immune in this state.

The creature howled as the barrage of energy burned at its exposed limbs. It seemed to be working.

Even Taro used his powers—he induced the creature's bones to rapid growth, causing its right arm to buckle sickeningly.

When the Tarbizhad laughed, Cheska shuddered, a chill coursing through her entire body. It had laughed, as if their combined powers were a humorous attempt at resistance

Cheska spotted the creeping, red tendrils spreading over Titus's body. In a handful of heartbeats, Titus's arms went limp and he no longer held the Tarbizhad— the Tarbizhad held him.

"No!" Felicia screamed, sending a burst of telepathic energy that echoed in the minds of the entire team.

The Tarbizhad winced, still holding Titus like a

shield.

"Cheska, you can do this," Taro said. As if he expected her to stop time again. She couldn't. She was wrecked, like a marathon runner who'd broken both ankles getting across the finish line—what did he expect of her?

"We-," he touched her gauntlet, "can do this. Together."

She understood. She removed her gauntlet, as did Taro. They held hands and she felt his healing power wash over her like a warm rain. The sensation was so intense, so pleasurable, she had to catch her breath. "*Wow*," she whispered, exhilarated.

Cheska Bellamy stopped time, freezing the Tarbizhad. She didn't stop there—she flexed time, like one might flex a thin piece of steel between their fingers—back and forth, back and forth. The Tarbizhad began to ripple and twitch. It wasn't laughing now.

As she felt her cells bursting under the exertion, she also felt the power of Taro's touch countering it.

Cheska's heart began to race as time fluttered for the Tarbizhad, bending, and twisting it. Faster and faster, until it began to oscillate and vibrate. Cheska gave one final scream, "Die!"

Its head and all four limbs were torn from its body, striking the walls of the terraforming plant.

Cheska collapsed.

Best Laid Plans

LIKE A COOL MIST FALLING on its face, awareness returned. Its senses awakening to the incoming data. There was only one reason it would have been revived—their First was dead.

From its cocoon, the Tarbizhad gazed across the core of the hive—a great globe of shadow. Countless, writhing forms lined the walls of the dark sphere.

They were awakening.

***

Cheska came-to in the infirmary, bright lights and white walls a stark contrast to the shades of red on the planet's surface. Dr. Mavros stood over her.

"What happened?" She asked.

"Appears that you collapsed, young lady," he said.

"Titus?" she asked.

Dr. Mavros shook his head.

Cheska squeezed her eyes shut, wishing she could loop back and fix things.

Dr. Mavros placed a hand on her shoulder. "Taro tried. Nothing he could do."

A sense of dread swept through her in nauseating waves. What had she done? She damn well knew— she'd gotten two of the Metahumans killed, that's what.

When Cheska opened here eyes, Delfina stood in the room. She hadn't wanted to see Delfina's scowling face, but she knew it had to come, knew she'd be punished— or worse, for her- her what? Her attempt at actually doing something? How dare she feel indignant! At least Delfina had kept these people alive.

"How are you feeling, Cheska?" Delfina asked.

"Weak, but ok … considering."

Delfina nodded but said nothing. She just stared at Cheska with eyes that seemed to be calculating Cheska's worth versus her cost. That's what Cheska would be doing after all. Maybe not a few weeks ago, but with the memories of an entire planet in her head, she had a new perspective on life.

"Hey there, kiddo!" Jak said as he bounded in to the infirmary.

Cheska lost any pretense of bravery and sobbed. "Jak," she said with a whimper.

Jak put his arms around her. He didn't judge her, he just comforted her. "It's all right, kiddo. You're ok."

"But- Titus? Zula?" Cheska pleaded.

"I know. But you killed a Tarbizhad. Nobody's ever done that," Jak said with an approving tone. He nodded to Delfina, as if prompting her.

Delfina nodded. "I suppose that is a small victory. We're going to make another engrammatic serum from the Tarbizhad's brain. They have genetic memory, which is where our benefactors borrowed the ability to gift you and Taro with the human memories. We'd like to give you both those memories as well. That could help the Aoratos in ways we can't even begin to imagine."

"Anything!" Cheska said, desperate to make up for the loss of her teammates—not that she ever could. She'd carry the weight of their deaths as heavily as she would the Watcher she'd gunned down on the *Ghimorphos*. She wished they could pluck those memories out, and she thought Delfina probably could, but she would never do that. Those memories—that guilt—was the burden she had to bear.

"Cheska," Delfina said, "whatever you learn, keep to yourself. Felicia and I will debrief you afterward. We need to maintain tight control on what this Tarbizhad knows."

***

Cheska and Dr. Foehner sat in the cafeteria, both nursing a cup of tea.

"I'm proud of you," Dr. Foehner said.

Cheska smiled weakly. "Thanks."

"You would have kicked ass in my gravitics department."

"Yeah, I would have." Cheska

"You think Delfina is ever going to forgive me for not revealing the beacon?" Dr. Foehner asked, changing the topic.

Cheska shrugged. "She's an angry woman. I don't get what Jak sees in her."

"I'm sure she's a different woman from the girl he paired with twelve-years ago. Running the resistance has to be- "

Brrramp! Brrramp! Brrramp! Brrramp! Brrramp! Brrramp! A familiar klaxon shattered the silence.

Cheska's stomach tightened and her libs felt chilled.

"Intruder alert?" Dr. Foehner asked.

Cheska was already on her feet. She tapped her wristcomm, about to contact Titus, then switched channels to Jak. "Jak, location?"

"Infirmary, on my way now," he responded.

When Cheska arrived at the infirmary she found Jak bent over Dr. Mavros, who lay prone on the floor. Another guard stood by the door.

"What happened?" Cheska asked.

With Jak's help, Dr. Mavros sat up, looking dazed. He had laceration across his face. He shook his head slowly. "Not sure. Somebody hit me. That's all I remember."

"Taro." Cheska remembered that he was here working. She bolted across the infirmary, looking beside beds and medical equipment. Then she found him.

"No!" Cheska screamed. Taro lay completely still, red veins crisscrossing his face, eyes bulging milky white. She fell to the floor, gathering up his head with her hands.

"Lock down the base!" Jak ordered. "We've got another assassin."

Felicia and Delfina both entered the infirmary at the

same time.

Cheska caught sight of Delfina and exploded. She slowed time enough so that Delfina could see her coming, see Cheska's hand, reaching for her throat. In a flash she had Delfina in a death-grip. "You killed him!" she screamed.

Delfina tried to resist, but Cheska rippled time, causing Delfina to howl as parts of her body aged at different rates.

"Cheska! Stop it!" Felicia shouted.

"She killed Taro!"

"No. She didn't," Felicia said.

Dr. Foehner ran into the infirmary. "Cheska!"

Cheska looked back at Delfina and only then realized she had her knife at the woman's throat, its edger just pressing hard enough to draw a line of blood. Without taking her eyes off Delfina, she asked Felicia, "How do you know?"

Felicia showed her, projecting the thoughts directly into Cheska's mind. Delfina had been in the Control Center, and had nothing to do with Taro's death.

Cheska released Delfina, letting her slump to the floor.

This couldn't be happening. No, she wouldn't let it happen! She picked herself up off the floor and strode to Taro's body. She knelt beside him and stroked his cheek, then steeled herself—she knew this would hurt.

With every neuron she could muster, she jumped backward in time. One second. Two seconds. Three seconds. Each jump straining her a little more. Every jump felt like she was leaping over a bottomless chasm where she wasn't sure she'd make it—invoking a chilled feeling and a sense of vertigo. Four seconds, then five seconds. The coppery taste of blood registered—her nose was bleeding freely, her head swayed. Six seconds, then seven seconds. Her stomach churned, but she held on, jumping, jumping. The people in the room vanished as she skipped across time faster—sixty-seconds, then three minutes. Taro had vanished too. Five minutes— now Dr. Mavros reappeared in the infirmary—he stood near some medical equipment. She spotted Taro slumped over a bed above her, about to fall to the floor. Seven-minutes. Taro was on his feet, struggling with- Dr. Mavros? Red veins had extended from Dr. Mavros's hands and were snaking across Taro's face.

Eight minutes—Dr. Mavros was frozen mid-stride as he was walking toward Taro from across the infirmary.

Cheska let the bubble of time collapse. Dr. Mavros stopped with a look of confusion on his face. "Cheska?" He had time to say, before glancing down to stare at the plasma burn in his guts.

Cheska stood, arm extended, and had fired at his center of mass—just as she'd been taught.

Dr. Mavros slumped to his knees clutching his belly.

"Cheska!" Taro screamed. "What have you done?" Taro lunged toward Dr. Mavros and cupped his hands on the man's stomach. "Hold on, Doc, I've got you."

"He killed you," Cheska said evenly.

Taro looked back at her with an expression part confusion and part horror. He turned back to healing Dr. Mavros.

***

Cheska watched as Felicia stood over Dr. Mavros, who now lay sedated and recovering from his wounds. Felicia held his hand, her eyes closed, with a pained expression on her face. She pulled away suddenly, shuddering.

"That piece of- " Felicia scowled. "It's all true, what Cheska said. He's a Venator—a hunter-killer. He killed the other Venator here in the infirmary … a friend of his, called Osgar. Apparently Osgar had a change of heart when Delfina showed him who he was really serving. Osgar was planning to tell us about Dr. Mavros."

Delfina looked to be in a state of shock. "He's been here for years … Felicia, how could you not have sensed what he was?"

"Not my fault, boss," Felicia said, "that's what they were designed for. Stealth, hunting, and killing. Like the Voces, these Venator are part Tarbizhad. I suspect his defenses are down because he was wounded, otherwise we'd never have known."

Delfina vomited all over the glossy tile floor.

***

Cheska sat in the tiny side-garden she and Taro frequented. She slumped down in the seat and absently stroked the vine that Taro had made tickle her only days earlier. He was working an extra shift in the infirmary, since they were now short one doctor, and the other staff had to pick up the slack. Now was time for her—time to sit quietly and reflect, meditate. That made her think of Yog- "

"Ms. Bellamy?" came a woman's voice.

Cheska turned slowly. It wasn't a woman that Cheska

recognized, but then, there were over six-thousand people living here.

"I'm sorry. I want to be alone right now."

"I know, and I apologize for the intrusion, but it's urgent I speak with you." The woman sat down in Taro's spot.

"I believe I can help you in the days to come," she said. The woman's skin began to ripple and Cheska jumped up, her hand on her pistol.

"No! I mean you no harm," the woman said, hands raised.

Her skin darkened from tan to a shining cerulean blue. Cheska gasped. Her features were no longer human—still humanoid, but only vaguely.

"What are you?" Cheska demanded.

"According to the Tarbizhad, *I* am a demon. In the same way they called you an Abhuman, or deviant. Your people know my species as Skads. We are more properly know as the Skaduwee."

Cheska stood with her mouth agape, hand still on her pistol.

"My name is Modry," the Skaduwee said. "I'm the leader of the resistance, the Aoratos Prime—Delfina's … boss? I believe that's the word? I'm here to help."

***

Cheska sat astride a gravbike, hovering a couple of thousand meters above the ruddy plains, staring out across Krijese, remembering the first time she'd taken in this view, her arms around Taro. She glanced up to see the red starlight of Thorantis reflecting off the *Ghimorphos* high in orbit. She wondered what was happening to her mother. She felt bad that she'd hardly spared her mother a thought for days, but then, she had been running for her life.

Cheska considered her challenges; she had a group of Aoratos rebels hiding in an underground bunker; a broken planet with an atmosphere that wasn't breathable by the Indigens or her people; a single shapeshifting Skaduwee ally; and a starship in orbit with her people enslaved by a race of genetically engineered super-weapons. Oh, and … she and Taro were supposed to birth a line of Metahumans to drive back the Tarbizhad. Yeah, that was about the sum of her current burden.

She knew she had no time for self-pity. She'd had a choice, and she'd made it. These were her people, and she and Taro were their best chance to reclaim their freedom from the Tarbizhad. She started up into the heavens, feeling the sheer weight of numbers of all the stars pressing down on her. She felt heavy. Tired. She was just a girl. Only sixteen-years-old.

Could she help save humanity?

EPILOGUE

AS THE HORDE OF TARBIZHAD clambered up the walls and through the tunnels of the hive, nine shafts of pale light began to converge at the center of the hive.

The doors were opening. The contest had begun.

***

The Ngome City Confab had given Eliza Bellamy two weeks to grieve the loss of her daughter, Cheska. It hadn't been enough, but work had to get done, the ship had to continue its mission. Her heart ached every second of every minute. Losing her husband had been very hard—losing her daughter too … She continued examining the water feed into the 104'th floor penthouse of tower-12. There was something not working here, and she had to fix it. She caught a glimpse of their star, Thorantis, beginning its nightly dip below the horizon of Krijese.

She kneeled down to remove an access panel near the floor.

The worse part of this personal horror, were the claims that Cheska had been a deviant. How? How could that even be possible? Maybe Eliza was to blame? After her husband had died she'd lost her zest for life— for a while anyway. Perhaps the lack of attention to Cheska had led to her straying from the Covenant. What could she have done differently?

She set the access panel down then pressed her back to the wall and slumped onto the floor. As Eliza sat, staring out the window, she remembered how much pleasure this view used to give her. Seeing Ngome City from this 312 meter vantage had always been breathtaking … not today. It just reminded her that Cheska was gone.

A loud click sounded. The lights in the penthouse went dark.

"Great," Eliza muttered, "first the water, now the power." She shook her head and stood. Angry that her self-pity had been interrupted.

The apartment was still lit up from the lights in the adjacent buildings. Walking to the floor-to-ceiling windows, her mouth hung open. Throughout the city, lights cascaded off, like dominoes falling. In seconds the city was nearly consumed by darkness. Night was falling on Krijese. Soon even the trickle of light from Thorantis would be gone.

'Damn, this would be serious,' she thought. She tapped

her wristcomm to contact the Confab, but the device was dead. She tapped several more times—nothing. She was about to head to the stairs when a reverberating sound shook the windows. Somewhere between a screech and a howl, followed by a series of heavy ticks that she felt, rather than just heard. She shivered. Goosebumps exploded across her skin.

She picked her way to the windows to see what was happening below. The city was dark. She'd never seen it like this. In fact, as far as she knew, the city had never lost power in its history. She caught an ebony form streak amid the grey shadows. Eliza could just make out the shapes of people on the streets below. They were running. From what? That made no sense. With almost no light, people should be sitting still and waiting for engineering to get all systems back on line.

Screams. More screams. An ebony flash struck someone, tearing at it. It wasn't just another shadow—it was a thing—a creature. On other streets the horror was repeated. People ran screaming, dark forms preying on them.

"Great Savior, what's happening?"

- - - This is NOT the end - - -

Enjoy the story? Want the next installment FREE?
Consider leaving a review on Amazon
Follow this link www.goo.gl/blJ24p to post your review, then e-mail me the link to the review when you're done and I'll send you the next book when it's ready!

Hugh B. Long